Houseboy Rules

a Brazen Boys story

by Daryl Banner

Books By Daryl Banner

The Beautiful Dead Trilogy:

The Beautiful Dead	*(Book 1)*
Dead Of Winter	*(Book 2)*
Almost Alive	*(Book 3)*

The OUTLIER Series:

Outlier: Rebellion	*(Book 1)*
Outlier: Legacy	*(Book 2)*
Outlier: Reign Of Madness	*(Book 3)*
Outlier: Beyond Oblivion	*(Book 4)*
Outlier: Five Kings	*(Book 5)*

The Brazen Boys:

A series of standalone M/M romance novellas.

Dorm Game	*(Book 1)*
On The Edge	*(Book 2)*
Owned By The Freshman	*(Book 3)*
Dog Tags	*(Book 4)*
All Yours Tonight	*(Book 5)*
Straight Up	*(Book 6)*
Houseboy Rules	*(Book 7)*

Other Books by Daryl Banner:

super psycho future killers
Psychology Of Want
Love And Other Bad Ideas
(a collection of seven short plays)

Houseboy Rules: a Brazen Boys story

Copyright © 2015 by Daryl Banner

All rights reserved.

This book is a work of fiction.
Names, characters, groups, businesses, and incidents either
are the product of the author's imagination or are used
fictitiously. Any resemblance to actual places or persons,
living or dead, is entirely coincidental.

Cover & Interior Design : Daryl Banner

Cover Model : Nick Duffy
www.instagram.com/nickduffyfitness

Photo of Nick Duffy by Simon Barnes

Houseboy Rules

a Brazen Boys story

by Daryl Banner

[1]

When he peels the shirt off, a chorus of dancing abs come out for a show. They ripple like the skin of some predatory, slithery snake. His hand runs up his body all clumsy-like, bumping along each of his abs and past his odd Florida-shaped birthmark until they discover a nipple, which he gives a pinch.

"Like what you see?" he moans, grinning stupidly. He pops his left pec, his right pec, gives me a playful wiggle of his eyebrows.

I'm so fucking bored.

"Try another song," I suggest to him tiredly. "This crap you're playing is so retro-pop, I feel like I'm stuck at some gay club 90's hell."

His seduction act dropped in an instant, he moves to the laptop and flips through a few songs. I wait, lying on the king-size bed with my back propped up by six feather pillows. I wear a modest white tee and lilac silken pajama pants. I watch as he picks his perfect song, muscular and naked save for his knee-length white boxer-briefs. His hair is as pale as his skin, and terribly groomed. Normally I'd find that hot, but today I just find it lazy. I mean, this is a boy desperately working for his tip. Shouldn't he have, perhaps, gazed at a mirror at some point in the past hour?

"Nice, yes," he decides, arriving at some odd indie-techno track. "This will do." Not that he asks me whether or not I concur.

All the money in the world can't buy someone good taste.

He resumes his striptease where he'd left off with a hand at his nipple, pinching. Climbing onto the end of the bed, he gets on his knees and starts to moan, working his nipple. He does the porn star half-gasp, lips parting like a goldfish.

"Please don't moan."

He stops, smiles, then continues in silence. His eyes rock back into his head and he bites his lip, tickling his nipple with his finger while I watch tiredly. I always expect the boys to read my mind, all my houseboys. I expect them to know what I want. I have high expectations. But all the money in the world can't buy someone a personality.

Watching him work, I think about all the people in the world who go on actual dates. I think about the men who don't have to surround themselves with pretty boys that they've paid for. I think about what life would be like if, instead of us playing around in a bed with a hefty paycheck waiting on the nightstand, we were at a restaurant staring into each other's eyes over candlelight and a gentle conversation, waiting on our steaks to arrive. Do I even know what that kind of romantic life feels like?

Do I want to?

"Come here," I tell him, trying not to make it sound like the command it was.

Like some robot who's been switched from one setting to another, he abandons his nipple and crawls across the bed. To my side now, he perches on his knees again and stares down at me, waiting for another direction. *They always want to be directed*, I complain to myself. *They don't have minds of their own. The prettier they are, the less they think they have to do.*

"You want to put your hands on me?" he asks, then bites his lip again, running a hand up his body. His hand seems to be the one getting all the action in the room.

"Yes," I decide, bringing my own hand to join the party. When I touch his abs, I find myself surprised with how firm they are. My fingers tracing upward, they reach his chest and I start to breathe deeper. His pecs are tight, toned, not too big. He's a slender muscle boy, smooth and long in shape. "Yes," I repeat, and my other hand joins the first. Both my hands feel his body, exploring with growing delight.

"Good, good," he says, noting my found-at-last satisfaction. "I like your hands on me."

"I like my hands on you, too."

"Where else do you like them?" He reaches down, pecs squeezing together as his hands meet to pull down his underwear. I feel a wave of hunger, my hands enjoying it. "Want my cock?"

It's sort of like being in a buffet line with your friend, and while you're drooling over the bread rolls, he offers you a chicken nugget.

"Turn over," I tell him.

The confusion on his face is short-lived. He makes to say something just when I get to *my* knees, spin him around, and push his face into my 2,000 thread count Egyptian cotton sheets.

"Is this a bad time to discuss and reevaluate your employment?" I ask as I tug on his boxer-briefs, revealing his firm ass.

"Oh." His voice is muffled. "Is this about the dishes? I thought Madison was gonna do them and he didn't, so then Jason—"

"No. This isn't about dishes." I jerk myself.

When my dad died, I wasn't told for a week. I thought he went on a vacation to somewhere called Heaven, and my mom just cried and cried for days. Her tears are my only memory of dad, other than the photos she kept showing me. I was four. When she remarried to a billionaire named Ernest, my life took a quick left turn and I would never understand love again. I went to elementary school in a town car every day. The kids made fun of me and my high-dollar shoes and all the things my new dad Ernest kept buying me to show his love—or, rather, to win my pretty mother's heart and spoil me to the dirty core. Money is love, that's the first lesson I learned. When a group of six kids cornered me to beat me up one day at recess, I offered them all a ride home in my town car. I was ten and I just learned my second most important lesson: Money is friendship. Money is respect.

Money is power.

Middle school and high school reinforced this dark and wonderful lesson. I bought every friend I had. Lunches were always on me. By this point, my stepdad was sick of me bringing the pretty boys home—not wanting anything to do with my *disgusting habits*—and while my mom turned a pretty blushed cheek to all my shenanigans, I continued to earn my allowance of approximately a limitless amount of cash a week with which I'd buy more friends, more lovers, and more respect. College sent me into a spiral of drugs and forbidden pleasures and paid-for test takers and paper writers, and too soon Ernest handed off a company to me. *Take it*, he said. *It basically runs itself. Take it and take the house. Your mother and I are moving to Argentina.*

Somewhere in the darkness of my soul, my real dad is watching from a vacation home in Heaven. Eating glumly from a bowl of Heaven's popcorn, he wonders where it all went wrong.

"Am I being fired?" His whimpering voice pulls me from my memories.

"The problem is," I blurt out, annoyed as I idly glance around for the renegade lube, "I can't get hard right now, and I'm way too young to have erectile dysfunction." We'll ignore the fact that I'm pushing forty-two and, despite my somewhat youthful face, I'm *not* the spritely boy I used to be. "Something is clearly lacking."

He doesn't respond, not even with one of his fake porn star moans. He seems stirred up, lost in thought, apprehensive.

"Let's face it, Oliver. You've had a nice time here for the last—three months, has it been? I've paid you well," I point out, still jerking my cock in vain, "but some things just aren't meant to be." The proverbial breakup speech. It's not you, it's ... well, you.

"Is there ... Is there anything I can ... do?"

Already acting like the dumped ex. "No."

He casts his eyes down, a shamed dog. I can see his mind working out where he's gone wrong. Maybe it *is* me. A beautiful man's ass is pressed into my thighs, ready, and I still can't get hard. I'm jerking, annoyed, but uninspired. All the money in the world can't buy a boner.

Well, technically not. "Need some help?" he asks reluctantly.

"I need a sandwich," I decide, giving up and hopping off the bed.

"W-What do I do now?" he asks from the bed in half a whimper, the dreadful indie-pop still pop-pop-popping from the laptop. *Pack your things,* I think to myself, but won't dare tell him. I'll have one of my other boys tell him the news. What else do I pay them all for but to do my dirty work?

"I'm bored," I mutter. "Bored and boring."

And I'm hollow, I might add.

And I'm perpetually unsatisfied, I'm unhappy, and I make for miserable company, I might add.

My dead dad would be so proud of me.

I dismiss boys that no longer excite me like they're nothing but cum-laden tissues. I have no friends that look me in the face anymore; they all look at my wallet. I have approximately limitless cash, limitless time, and a company that runs itself. Thank you, Ernest.

Bored and boring.

I descend the spiral staircase to the den. Padding across the cold white tiles of my quieter-than-usual mansion, I pass through the spacious living room where two of my boys are playing the PS4, the image of their game projected on the wall. I didn't realize how annoyingly glued to that machine they'd be, otherwise I might've second-guessed buying it for them. "Pres," I call out.

Preston lifts up from the couch, a head of messy bleached-blonde hair, his bright green eyes sparkling. "Yes? Hungry?"

"Not for *le cock*." I take a seat at the bar.

Quick as a cat, shirtless, muscular Preston hops off the couch—leaving whatever character he was playing to die in a cacophony of aliens and gunfire—and strolls into the kitchen. He's got on pale blue jeans that he basically lives in, the bright white waistband of his designer briefs I bought him peeking out the top. I made it a rule for him to wear those jeans and go shirtless as often as possible. Seriously, it should be a crime to cover up such a display of muscle. He's got this cute way his hair curls in the front, dimples that go on for days, and whenever he looks at me, he speaks directly into my eyes, intense, focused, knowing. He seduces me at a glance. He's the smartest, being almost college educated, and always knows what I want.

Swinging open the fridge, he glances back just in time for me to say, "Sandwich, please. Turkey and brie."

"Only because you said 'please'," he teases, giving a wink, then pulls out some stuff. "Hope you weren't looking for a late night training after you eat," he adds, whipping out a couple slices of bread from the pantry. "I heard Kyle's staying the night at his girlfriend's."

Kyle's the one very-decidedly heterosexual houseboy I employ. He doubles as my trainer. Though I expect *some* form of sexual satisfaction from all my boys, just the *sight* of Kyle is enough. He's built like a stallion, his chest huge and sculpted, nipples threatening to poke holes in those athletic compression tops he always has on. Let us not even *begin* to discuss the work of art that is his ass in those signature black Under Armour gym shorts of his. If I could give him a two-thousand dollar raise just to lay a single hand on that, I so would. *I've tried.* He's my deepest wish among all the boys. But money, I've come to learn, only moves things from one hand to another; it isn't always known to grant wishes.

"Do you think I'm an awful person?" I ask Preston's smooth, muscled chest as he prepares my sandwich, noting how his pecs pull tight in the middle, his form more lithe and triangular than the others. *My food-making panther*, I used to call him. He knows to face me while preparing food. That way, I get the best view.

Preston's face wrinkles. "Why would you ask that?" His bright green eyes meet mine. I bought him those eyes. Contacts. "'Course not. You're generous. Give us a place to live. You got my buddy Madison out of a bad situation. Tell me who's calling you awful, I'll whip their ass."

"I am."

He bites his lip. "Well, then. Guess I'm gonna have to ... whip your ass." He gives me a wink, which I return with a grateful smile. Preston always knows what to say.

The finished sandwich set neatly in front of me on a plate with dolphins etched around the rim, Preston comes around the counter with a cloth dinner napkin and lays the thing across my lap. "Thanks," I make sure to say. "You always know how to take care of me, Pres."

"Oh, I only do it 'cause you pay me," he says, and I have to laugh. It's the first real laugh I've had all day. "You're the man of the house," he adds with a shrug. "You get whatever it is you want. Just snap your fingers and it's yours."

I snap my fingers. "I want something to make my heart flutter."

He grins knowingly, then brings his face to mine, laying a soft kiss on my lips. As promised, my heart flutters and I feel the electric thrill that hours with what's-his-name upstairs could not provide. I even feel my cock stir beneath my dinner napkin like a shameful secret. Preston always smells so nice and his lips are as soft as his eyes. How's that possible? When he pulls away, he asks, "Anything else?"

"Marry me," I mutter.

He gives me a knowing look. "Well, well. Don't tease me now. You know I'd say yes."

"If I wasn't so sure you were marrying my

bank account, too," I say teasingly, though a very notable portion of my heart sinks when I utter the words, knowing the truth in them.

Preston wiggles his nose. "Come back at me when you're ready to bend a knee." He hovers for a bit at the counter, his green eyes floating near mine. After a few seconds have passed, I suppose he figures the moment's ended, and he gives a little wink before turning about and returning to his and Jason's game in the other room.

I stare after him, reminded suddenly of our time together last week when, over the course of an hour, an innocent lesson in how to make fudge turned into a sticky session of chocolate-body-licking, cock-sucking, and cumming on the kitchen floor. Oh, the mess we had to clean up. I recall fondly the shower afterwards as well, and the slick touch of his body ...

I'm not always so reckless.

After eating no more than two bites of this delicious gourmet turkey and brie that Preston's prepared for me, I spot Oliver descending the stairs. He eyes me anxiously, gives a meek nod, then disappears into the den. Ugh. I still have to tell one of the boys to terminate him. Seeing that boy skulking around just depresses me. Already I'm limp as a worm again.

In the shadowy recesses of my mind, I start to hear all the words that I'd just said to him all over again ... and those good feelings I was just having start to turn sour.

Sometimes, I get so sick of myself.

I think of happily married couples. I think again about the thrill of two people on a date. I think about love stories on TV and passionate romance books and some desperate guy saving up all his hard-earned cash so he can afford a prostitute to fulfill his fantasies on a special Saturday night. Here I am, swallowed up in a mansion the size of twenty houses and I literally have seven hot, adorable fantasies living with me. If I looked into my life from the outside, I would see a sad, pathetic fucker with buckets of money who gave up seeking real happiness and decided, instead, to buy it.

What Preston said was a joke, but there's a ring of truth in it: he's only here because I pay him. Oliver too. Kyle, my straight trainer. Jason. Madison. Stefan. Zac. Like so many others I've had work for me, some of these boys will move on. Some of them will stick around longer, sure, but they don't really belong to me.

They're paid for.

I won't kid myself and say it doesn't do them some good. Most of these boys are lost. Wandering souls. Little or no family. Figuring things out. Poor Madison, he was kicked out of his house after his parents found out he'd done a gay porn. He was just trying to pay for a car. He's Preston's friend—lanky, messy hair that looks cute on him—and it was through Preston that I heard of his plight, then soon after hired him. Madison's now my unofficial pool boy and handyman, despite not being particularly skilled in either thing. I have to remind myself they're getting something out of this, too. They have a home, rent-free, and I pay them steady.

But something's still missing.

Amidst my mental torture, my eyes wander to a stack of applicants I'd left on the counter. I bring the top folder to me, curious. I open it, then toss the applicant aside, bored at once. I open the next, find two dead eyes staring into mine. *Not in the business of hiring zombies,* I tell myself. I pull open the next, then say, "Next."

It isn't until I reach the seventh in the pile that my eyes grow huge. I'm gazing at the most adorable boy I've ever seen. I stop chewing at once, taken hostage by his bright blue eyes, his unexpectedly dark and spiky hair, his full lips and flushed cheeks. He needs money for college and has experience in housesitting and dogsitting from watching his neighbor's. *I'll be your dog,* I think, watching his gorgeous eyes. It's one of those fall-instantly-in-love sort of things. I imagine all the high school dances I could've asked him to, if we were born at the same time. I imagine being his best friend, having a life with him. I want him to be my best friend and my lover. Oh, look, he also weightlifts and does lawns, and he wants to be a doctor someday.

All my worries are dowsed away in an instant. "Zac," I call out, unable to pull my eyes away from the applicant's face. *I want to be a doctor someday,* he says on his application. *I want to save lives and, as corny as it sounds, I like the idea of fixing people.* "Zac," I call again, desperate. Finally, the tall and ever-stoic white-blonde boy rushes down the stairs, arriving at the kitchen half-dressed and out of breath. "There you are," I say without hardly even looking at him. "Please tell Oliver to pack up his things. We're sending him on his way. Get Jason to cut him a check, he knows how. I'll sign it."

"Oh." Zac grunts, still rubbing the sleep out of his eyes. "That's it?"

I give him an eager smile, handing off the folder. "And call this one in the morning," I tell him. "We're hiring a new houseboy."

[2]

Just watching the way he lounges in my limo, I know I picked the perfect one.

He's twelve times more adorable than his photo. *Twelve times.* Big blue eyes. Pitch black hair, short and tousled. His nose is a button. He looks at everything with wonder. I can only imagine what he's thinking after the offer I made him. He must think he's won the lottery.

And he has, really.

"I wasn't expecting a limo." He lifts a thick black eyebrow, his sparkling blue eyes drifting to the bar at his side, entranced. "Wow."

I smile. "Help yourself."

"Oh." The smile he makes brightens his face. His teeth show white against his flushed, boyish cheeks. "Thanks, Liam. That's your name, right?"

"Call me whatever you want."

Despite his sinewy figure, this boy's arms are impossibly thick and defined. Every tiny effort he makes, whether to care for an itch on his nose or to adjust himself on that seat across from me, causes his arms to flex beautifully. I can hardly keep my eyes off of them.

"I can't wait to meet the boss," he admits.

"We'll arrive soon." He doesn't know *I'm* the boss who's interviewing him. "Quite soon."

Not to mention the glimpse of his ass I caught when he bent over to get into the limo. In that instant, his tight, baby blue polo lifted to give me the sweetest wink of his taut lower back muscles and the tops of two firm ass cheeks peeking out of his low-hanging jeans. He has one of those plump butts you want to grab the instant you lay eyes on it. I'm sick with sexual hunger and I've hardly been in his presence for more than six minutes.

"Have you met him?" he asks, anxious. "Is there anything I should know ahead of time? I heard he's gay. I heard he's gay and he likes young guys. That's an advantage for me, right? That's gotta be a total advantage."

He's only eighteen, fresh out of high school, innocent as a kitten—a big, cute-faced muscular kitten with crystalline blue eyes. That fact, admittedly, makes me far more sad than excited. What if I corrupt him? He's so sweet. He's so unknowing. He's so soft.

"A considerable advantage," I confess.

"Right on." He takes a deep breath, exhales, then licks his lips.

I've never craved someone this young before. I didn't even care to note his age until he was already called and the interview set up. By the look of his body, you'd say he's twenty-something, but the youth is given away by his baby face. *He's so lucky*, I tell myself. He might as well open my wallet up and help himself.

"Why'd you apply for the job?" I ask.

He gives the question a moment of thought. "Flexibility of hours," he says. "I also like that it's not just one thing I'm being hired for. The job almost sounds like a personal assistant type of job. Is that what I'm gonna be?"

"If you pass the interview."

"Right, right," he agrees. "The interview."

He might not trust any of this just yet, but he will soon enough. There's nothing like the green power of cash to ease a boy's hesitation.

"Tastes nice," he says after taking a little sip from a glass of wine he just poured himself. He nods casually, glancing out the window, and I have to wonder if he's ever even drank a drop of alcohol in his life. *Of course he has*, I tell myself, feeling dumb. *Not everyone's as innocent as they look.* Still ...

"It's three hundred dollars a bottle," I point out. "I sure hope it tastes nice."

He hesitates before his next sip, staring at the contents of his glass as though it'd become some frightful vision. Then he recovers, flashes me a smile and says, "Bottoms up."

I lean back and watch him as he sips on my three-hundred-dollar wine like a bottle of Pepsi. His arm flexes deliciously as he brings it to his lips. He chose to sit on the opposite side of the limo. That's wise; I get a better view of what I'm buying and he has a more advantageous position to sell what he's selling. Not that he realizes who he's selling to. With his legs spread the way some dude sits on a couch to watch Sunday football, I get an enticing view of his crotch, and I daresay it is *not* lacking.

"Does your boss being gay affect your desire to work for him?" I ask sincerely.

"No," he answers quickly, a fleck of wine soaring from his mouth. "Not at all. I'm really hard to shock. I'm open-minded. Raised that way, I guess. Hell, I'll even do all the work in my underwear if the boss wants."

Don't tempt me. I'll make that a new houseboy rule. "You have a lot of skills," I point out, subtly shifting the topic, "judging from your application. Tell me what you're best at." I've already done my research and had a connection of mine do a full background on this boy in my limo. I'm nothing if not thorough.

"Getting work done," he decides after half-choking on a mouthful of wine. "I never quit on a job, not ever," he goes on, staring at me with his eyes watering from the alcohol. "Whatever the task, I do it thoroughly and I leave no turn unstoned."

No turn unstoned. Freudian? Or is he that easy on the alcohol? "Aren't we lucky to have you, then," I jest with an endearing smirk.

"Yep!" He looks out the window.

Despite that proud and puffy muscular body of his, the look in his baby blue eyes is one of a timid boy trying to fit in with his older brother's cool friends, sipping that wine. His head nods, bobbing to some song that's not playing. He starts swirling the glass like some fancy wine taster, nearly losing some of it over the brim. *He's nervous*, I realize. There's a thick leather cuff on his wrist which might or might not be a watch—I can't quite tell. I also notice a stud in his left ear, glimmering in the light.

"You're really cute," I tell him suddenly.

He looks at me, startled as though I'd just said something very scary. Quickly, his face recovers, he puts on his best smile and says, "I'm your type, huh?"

He was told what this job would pay. He knows the money is real and that there's potential for enough to pay his tuition. He already feels "paid-for" even without being officially hired yet or getting his first paycheck ... and the pressure of what may be requested of him is overwhelming and scary. I see the fear in his blue watery eyes.

"I don't really have a type," I confess.

"So you ... just think I'm plain cute, huh?" He smiles anxiously, reluctantly takes another sip, coughs, licks a drop of wine off his lips. "You like my baby blues, huh?"

I laugh. "You have very nice eyes, that much is true. And you work out, clearly."

"Football in high school," he lies. He was a varsity wrestler. I can tell just by his cute cauliflower ears. "I hit the gym every day." He sips again and looks out the window, his eyes shimmering as they catch the glow of a passing streetlight. Suddenly, he laughs. "I always wanted to have a gay friend. Hey, you work for him, right? Wanna buddy-up if I get hired? Consider the perks: you get to be around my pretty face all the time."

I laugh while he flashes teeth, thinking himself clever. He is insanely adorable, even when he's so nervous he's likely to piss himself before we arrive. "Sounds like a deal."

"Great!" He wipes at a spot in the window.

"You ever been picked up in a limo before?"

"Oh, yeah," he says too quickly. "Sure. For prom." We both laugh. "This one's way bigger, though." He finishes off his glass, goes for another. *Slow down*, I want to tell him. *I need you thinking straight when we get to the house.*

"Prom," I echo, smiling as he sips from his new glass. *Try to make him comfortable. You could still lose him. He's playing it cool for now, but at any moment, a guy like this could just ...* "You have a great personality. That'll go a long way, should you be employed. Let me tell you a few things before we get there."

He rests the wine glass on his thigh, looks at me with a sudden loss of all humor, serious as a sapphire. He swallows hard. Eyebrows lifted, listening, he waits for my words.

I'm his best gay buddy now. He wants my advice. My words have become gold.

"You won't be asked to do anything," I tell him, "that makes you feel uncomfortable. You won't be pushed, persuaded, nor manipulated into doing anything out of your realm of comfort. We want you to feel totally at home. You're free to go at any time, no hard feelings."

He seems to take a few extra seconds to process what I said. Then he smiles and retorts, "Hopefully we have lots of ... *hard* feelings." He gives me a cheeky wink.

He's trying to convince me how cool and comfortable he is with all of this. But he's way nervous, has no idea what he's in for, and far away from home. He knows it. I know it. And he doesn't know I know it.

"It's important to understand," I reiterate.

"That I can back out of this?" He nods, presses his lips together into a pensive frown. "Yeah, okay," he agrees after a moment of what I take to be *actual* deliberation. "I accept that. Yeah. If the job turns out not to be, uh … a good fit or whatever, then we'll handle it like adults and I'll just … decline." He takes another gulp.

Watching his eyes sparkle, I realize picking up that application was the best thing I've done in months. "So, Evan," I say, leaning forward in my seat. "You want to … be a doctor?"

His eyes seem to sparkle at the use of his name, whether out of anxiety or kindness, I can't say. "Y-Yes. I like helping people."

"You like the idea of saving people. Fixing people. You put that in your application."

"Did I?" He chuckles. "Well, it's true."

"Is there anything you won't do?" I ask. "Any sort of … chores or … or kind of work that you would prefer not doing?"

He almost chokes on his swallow of wine. "Oh," he mutters after recovering. I swear, I didn't have a second meaning buried in my question; I was being sincere. "Yeah, uh. I draw the line at some of the ... grosser stuff. I mean, I'll stick my hand in a toilet if I gotta, but would prefer not to. Oh, I didn't even ask. Is my boss, like, ninety years old or something? I really don't wanna change bedpans." His leg starts to hop in place quickly. "Other than that, though, I'll do most other things."

Something tells me he has no idea the long list of crazy shit he could be implying with "most other things", but I'll resist commenting. I'm not interested in freaky stuff anyway. "You seem agile, quick. Also smart. I like how you dress," I tell him. "You seem like a very clean guy. The boss likes clean. He'll expect clean."

"I'm very, very clean," he insists, as if I still need convincing. "Squeaky." He flashes his teeth again, hiding all his nervousness with false confidence and cockiness.

It's adorable, really. "Boss's in his mid-thirties," I lie, praying it becomes true, as if I'll find a way to buy a decade of my life back.

"Oh, good. No bedpans." We share a light chuckle. "Thirties and gay. Does he have a guy? I don't wanna pull out the flirt if, like, it's gonna cause a problem, or ..."

"Bring the flirt," I tell him. "No boys in his life except the ones that work for him, and he's happy to have it that way." My eyes drift down to his knees, sickened by the ease with which these lies slip off my tongue. "He won't mind the flirting one bit." He laughs nervously into his glass, bubbles forming in the wine. "You're straight, but I take it you're ... open to ...?"

"Yeah, I'm straight," he asserts, despite the fact that his ex is a guy from his school's choir department. They broke up at the start of the summer and he hasn't dated since. My sources are reliable, though sometimes not so ethical. Money buys secrets, too. "Straight but open."

"You know, it's perfectly okay if you're not straight," I tell him. "You won't be hired based on your sexuality. There's a straight man that works for—for the boss." I almost gave myself away right then. "Just be yourself. Really, I think it's directness and honesty and truth that the boss so ..."—my eyes scan him: foot, to thigh, to crotch, to hips, to pecs, to shoulders, to lips, to eyes—"craves."

"I know what you mean," he says lightly, as if not noticing at all that my eyes just slid up his body like a pair of lusty fingers. "Maybe I'm more ... *open* ... than straight." He winks.

And more gay *than open*, I resist adding. "Do you have any dietary needs? The bag boy can pick you up whatever you want, should you take the job and move in."

"Bag boy?"

"He handles the groceries, keeps the pantry stocked, cooks ... and carries bags. The name just kinda stuck. It's silly. His name's Preston. He's really more like a live-in chef."

"How many ... houseboys ... work there?"

"Seven. Well, six," I correct myself, noting with due sadness the boy I just let go this morning. Oliver pleaded for me to keep him, but I was too busy being upstairs and not caring to be bothered with emotions. "At our highest point, there were eleven boys living in the house." A guy who notices the little things would've spotted the subtle flinch of surprise in his left eyebrow; I am such a guy.

"Eleven. Wow. But six right now, you said? A chef and, uh ..." He's sorting it in his head. "Who're the others? What do they do?"

"There's a trainer, Kyle. He keeps the boss in shape. He's straight and ... very *not* open." I laugh. Evan does as well, though it sounds a bit like he feels obligated to. "There's Stefan, the cleaning and laundry guy. Freckly, messy red hair, drinks a lot—an Irish frat boy. There's the driver Zac. He's driving us now, actually." I smile, finding it amusing as Evan spins to take a peek through the dividing window. "Don't worry, he can't hear any of this."

"Oh." Evan turns back to me, his eyes wide and curious. "All his employees live with him?"

"Yes."

"Do they all ... get in bed with him?" His grip on the wine glass is slipping. It half rests on his thigh, half hangs by his fingertips.

"No." I watch the glass. "The boss doesn't pay for, nor does he expect, sex from any of his houseboys." I gently exclude the fact that every boy under my roof has had every part of their body touched by my hands at some point. Even my dream-boy straight trainer Kyle gave in to my asking him if I could feel his biceps ... "for motivation," I'd assured him. Kyle sneered, but let me grip and admire his rock-hard baseball biceps anyway. It was short-lived but lovely.

"And what do *you* do?"

"Oh, this and that," I answer with a smile.

"So, this guy surrounds himself with hot young boys that ... take care of him ... and his house." He licks his lips, thinking. "If I were to get the job, then I'm basically, like, eye candy for this boss guy and, like, I'm probably going to be doing housework and getting ogled all summer long. Is that how this is going down?"

I laugh. He doesn't. "He's really a very nice guy," I say quickly, my laughter ceased. "Don't get the wrong idea. He's not as sleazy as he sounds, really. He's ..."

But am I? I can't even finish the sentence, overcome with the reality of my own life. Maybe I should've revealed my identity earlier. Maybe what Evan just said was a little bit ... *too* honest a portrayal of my sad, selfish life.

My dad's still watching me, kicking back in a beach recliner at a resort in Heaven, sipping a piña colada and squinting at me through a pair of oversized sunglasses, a dab of white suntan lotion on his nose.

"He's what?" Evan urges me to finish the sentence.

I meet his eyes. "Lonely."

"Oh." Evan bites his lip. "I guess I kinda got a certain impression after I was required to provide a drug test and ... and STD tests. It all seemed a bit more like ... like he might have been expecting, uh ..." Evan bites his lip again, gnawing. "My mom asked me what kind of job I was going for. I left out *a lot* of details. When I mowed lawns for a neighbor down the street for the past two summers—an old man—he'd always make me lemonade and then watch me from the front window. He thought I didn't notice but I did. I knew he watched me. When I did it shirtless, he'd pay more. Who knows what else he was doing. I guess I figured this job would be ... a bit like that, except ... maybe the boss would expect me to ..." He goes quiet and shuts his eyes, flustered and blushing.

"Sex isn't part of it, Evan," I assure him, perhaps with more force than I intend. He flips open his eyes. "You're not a prostitute. You're not being hired for sex." *Not that a simple raise or a little bump in your weekly pay won't convince you to please me.* I know how pretty boys work. I've paid for them my whole stupid life, ever since that day the boys tried to beat me up at recess. "You would be hired for simple housework and no more. Take my word for it. Nothing's ... Nothing else is expected of you."

I want to stare at his pecs bulging in that tight blue polo of his. I want to stare at his inviting crotch. I want to pounce on every inch of his muscular body, but I keep glued to his eyes and deny myself every impulse.

He sighs with relief, perhaps for the first time this whole limo ride. "Thanks, Liam. You really know how to put a dude at ease." He looks out the window, then becomes nervous all over again. "We're here already?"

"Almost." Evan looks at me, confused. "The driveway's long," I clarify with a smile.

Staring out the window, his lips parting, he looks something between awed and terrified. "Six others, huh?" Evan weighs that in his mind for a while. "Must be a big house."

"Practically a castle," I agree.

The garden lights flash across our faces as we curve down the road, and soon the front doors and brightly-lit windows to my property loom. Evan twists around to get a better view, his shirt lifting to give a peek of his flexed abs and slim, dimpled hips.

I distract myself by asking: "Ready?"

He turns to me, startled, then nods.

The driver comes around to let us out. I let Evan get out first, partly to be polite, partly because I enjoy the view of his ass as he moves by me, his tight little shirt sneaking up to give me a peek of his lower back once again. I follow him out and watch as his eyes drink in the sight of my mansion. Only two stories, somewhat squatty, but sprawling and enormous in reality. Even at night the lawn is a sea of shimmering green emeralds lit by garden lamps and glass lanterns that line the walkway to the front door, which in itself is quite massive, sandwiched by tall glass windows. The driver Zac, dressed in a sleeveless white shirt with a black bowtie, follows quietly behind—yes, I *do* require him to wear that sexy and ridiculous stripperesque uniform every time he drives me. Zac is a tall, stoic, strong-and-silent-type with white-blonde spiky hair. The limo keys jangle from his hand as he walks. I stay a step or two behind Evan because, well, the sight of his ass moving as he walks is about the most delicious thing I've seen in years. And I've seen lots.

He's not as sleazy as he sounds. I snap my eyes up, focused on the door and nothing else.

I'm my own joke and punch line.

Zac comes forward to open the front door to the house for us. Evan—blank-eyed, amazed, intimidated, maybe still a little buzzed—steps over the threshold to my castle (let's be honest) and seems stupefied, speechless as a stone. First thing, he looks up. *Everyone always looks up.* The entry hall is deceivingly tall with a pair of curved staircases ahead that lead to my nine bedrooms, two galleries, library, and spare game room. Evan seems to have forgotten how to put one foot in front of the other.

"Come in," I encourage him, strolling over to the bar at the kitchen. Preston and Jason are on the couch gaming, big surprise. "Preston! Come make a snack for our applicant. Evan, what do you like to eat? What's your taste? Pres makes a mean grilled cheese."

"I'm okay, I'm not hungry, really," he says quickly, then wrinkles his face, hearing me belatedly. "G-Grilled cheese?"

"Surprised?" I grin. "Expected something else? A platter of crackers, imported French cheeses and caviar? Pres can get you that, too."

Preston hops into the kitchen, a dashing smile crossing his face. "This is the applicant?" He faces him, his eyes bright and inviting. "Hi, I'm Preston."

"Evan." They shake hands. "I'm g-good. You don't have to, uh ... make me anything."

"You sure?"

Preston keeps smiling, giving Evan the up-and-down with his eyes. Clearly I'm not the only one impressed with the fresh scenery that Evan's providing.

"I'm fine, thanks."

"Suit yourself." He looks Evan over again, his eyes playful and light. "Are we officially official? You hired yet, buddy? When do you start, bub?"

"Oh, no. I still haven't had the interview. I'm here to meet the boss, actually."

Preston, smart as a bee, catches on to my game. "Ah. Well. I imagine, since you're here at the house, you ... must have made quite the impression already." He gives me a knowing look, then excuses himself back to the den.

Evan turns to me with a hundred questions in his eyes, more anxious than ever. I answer them all with a question of my own: "You were told the wage you'd get as the new houseboy. Is that an acceptable wage for your needs?"

He sputters: "Y-Yes. More than enough."

"The terms of your living arrangements were explained earlier. Accept those, too?"

"Yes, I do, but—"

"Then the job is yours, Evan. You start tomorrow." I smile, then help myself to a glass of water while Evan stands there confused, his lips sputtering for a word to say. "I can show you which room will be yours, if you'd like a tour now. Your things are still in the back of the limo, aren't they?"

"B-But what about the interview?"

"We already had it." I take a casual sip from my glass, then set it softly on the counter. "In the limo."

The whites of Evan's eyes flash. "But you're—" Then comprehension draws on his cute as fuck face.

"Liam Hightower," I finish for him. "Your new boss." His cute black eyebrows lift, his lips parting. He flushes intensely. "You alright?"

"I'll take that grilled cheese," he says with a meek smile.

[3]

The tour of my impressive estate takes about thirty minutes, and I don't even show him everything. *He's so adorable.* After he's eaten one of Preston's best, I show him the bottom floor rather quickly, as it's very open and spacious. Upstairs, he sees the various bedrooms, including the one in which he will be staying. His eyebrows might be permanently glued in a surprised expression, as his adorably overwhelmed eyes never lose their surprise. *I'm really going to like having this one around,* I tell myself when he stares in disbelief at the size and lavishness of his room.

The backyard opens to a sprawling sea of grass and cobblestone walkways. A shimmering pool with an attached fountain and hot spring rest under half a canopy of shaded glass. There is even a guesthouse across from it, which no one ever really uses, despite it being lightly furnished. It's like a nice birthday gift someone stows away on a shelf and forgets about.

"So what do you think?" I ask after the tour's over and we're lounging on a long stone bench on the back veranda.

"I think my summer's gonna be awesome," he answers, his eyes scanning me again, seeing me for the first time from my head to my toes. It's a strange sensation, to have someone *actually* looking at me. I haven't felt it in a long time. Too long. There's something about Evan that's different, something about the way he looks at my eyes and not at the gold in my pockets. I hardly have to buy him; he's sold. I think he's still in shock that a guy like me is his boss. I wonder if I should be flattered ...

What's "a guy like me" anyway?

He already came packed with a backpack of clothes and a small duffle bag of personal items. I made sure the boy who set up the interview prepared Evan for the possibility of immediate hire and moving-in. When he brings his things into his new bedroom, the look on his face makes the sweat and anxiousness of this whole thing worth it. I just lean on the doorframe, appreciating our new guest.

He looks up suddenly, as if caught in a thought or worry.

"Anything you don't have or didn't bring, we can get for you," I tell him, trying to stab a guess at whatever worry it is that just entered his mind. "Laptop. Clothes. Anything at all."

"Clothes? Yeah, if I even need any." Evan smiles teasingly. I grin, resisting the slight blush that's trying to take over my face as I imagine him wearing nothing at all. "I said dumb things in the limo."

"I'm judging you very badly for them, too."

"At least someone is." He smirks. I return the smirk with a playful one of my own, though he doesn't see it. "So you, uh ... really take care of your employees. L-Laptop?"

"I try." I smile back and resist licking my lips as his arms flex, reaching into his backpack to pull out some more clothes I can't wait to see him in—and out of.

Ugh. I close my eyes, willing myself to undirty my mind, which seems a bit like trying to bend time.

"I'll ... let you get settled in," I say. It takes a fuck-lot more effort than one might realize to dismiss a person like me from a room that houses a guy like this. "If you need anything else, anything at all ... just find me, or any of the other boys should be able to help you."

"Thanks, Mr. Hightower."

"Liam. Just Liam."

We smile at each other. It's a brief moment, but it's lovely. I wonder in this short moment if this was the best or worst choice I've made in all my years of rich boredom and meandering through life's convoluted maze. I so often wonder what the fuck my purpose is other than to spend money and to eat money and to get horny with money.

In this small moment, I vow to myself to not do to Evan what I've done with the others. *Evan is special*, I tell myself—or rather, try to convince myself, thinking on all the boys I've bought, all the friends I've bought, the company that runs itself and Ernest who gave me anything I wanted. Everything I want turns into a piece of gold: shiny, plain, possessed, coveted, and *worthless*. Evan is in a league far higher, far greater, far more precious than the other boys. Don't take him for another toy in the toy box; he must be *respected*.

I wonder, at what cost?

I excuse myself from Evan's bedroom and disappear into another. Jason and Madison look up from their laptops, startled by my sudden entry. They're seated on the bed side-by-side with their backs propped up by a spread of fluffy black pillows. Their brown beady eyes meet mine.

They know what I'm here for.

"Hope I'm not interrupting," I mutter, all the horniness I've been building up in Evan's presence threatening to unstitch my every seam. "I was hoping you two might be in the mood to ... get friendly?"

Madison's eyes seem to shrink, but Jason, his skin like a sea of velvety coffee I could swim in all day, takes the lead, knowing exactly what I want. As I drop onto the corner of the bed, the ever-smooth Jason massages Madison's long, willowy, peaches-and-cream skater-boy body, working the shirt over his neck and leaving him in a pair of tight-fitting blue and green plaid boxers I bought him. I slip my cock out of my pants, watching with unblinking eyes as the boys get friendlier by the second.

This is the only healthy way I've learned to medicate myself. After overdosing twice, both within a year of each other in my early thirties, I've traded drugs for twice as many boys. Now and then when I get excited and my heart skips a beat, I wonder suddenly if I'm going to die. If I keel over, I have to honestly wonder, would the boys steal away the money in my pockets *before* calling an ambulance?

"Madison needs help," I point out.

Laying Madison across the bed, Jason licks down the long body of his friend like a dog down a tasty treat that lasts forever, working his way to the dessert concealed within those tight undies.

I suddenly find myself far too much apart from them. Gently easing myself into this boy sandwich, I reach with my free hand and stroke Jason's smooth body, feeling his subtle yet taut muscles as they move and flex and contract while he massages and kisses Madison. As Jason stretches to reach different parts of his buddy's torso, his shirt slides up and I see his smooth ass. Drawn to it like new inspiration, I slip my hand down its curved, supple shape, drawing down his underwear with it. It slides down so easily, you'd think the boys were slicked with oil. Maybe I should make that a new houseboy rule. I'll be first to volunteer in the daily oiling.

Jason is about to pull Madison's boxers down when I quickly interject: "With teeth." After a quick glance at me, he corrects his near-grievous-error and, instead of boring fingers, pulls his buddy's underwear down with his teeth. Madison's long semi hops out, still in need of help. Jason's lips come to greet it, swallowing, and lending the much needed help.

Finding myself harder than I've been in weeks, I go to town on my own cock, stroking while I massage Jason's ass. Every stroke begs that one day, Evan would be one of these boys on this bed. Every jagged gasp that escapes my lips curses my hiring the all-too-beautiful, young, charming, sweet, sexy, strapping Evan.

Respect Evan. Respect Evan. He isn't a toy. He's not your toy.

He's not your toy.

When Madison unexpectedly cums onto Jason's lips, surprising him, I surprise myself with a heavy, hearty orgasm of my own, spewing it all over Jason's ass and backside. I moan and curl my toes, drawing circles and coils and squiggles of cum across him.

Jason and Madison stare at me, as if asking whether I'm satisfied. "Yes," I say, answering their unasked question. Then, I dismiss myself to my own room where a shower twice the size any shower ought to be awaits. I suspect they'll be taking an unplanned extra shower of their own, maybe together. I wonder for a moment if I ought to join them, then decide they've served me enough today.

See? I'm not so greedy. I'm good to the boys, and the boys are good to me.

Evan's training begins the next morning. I pair him up with the redhead maybe-Irish frat boy Stefan because Stefan's the youngest of the others—twenty, to be precise—and he'll give him the basics of how the house is kept up, what the common day-to-day chores involve, and where everything's located. I pull a laptop to the lounge couch near the window and check emails, mildly curious about the status of that company I run, while sneaking glances into the yard where Stefan's showing Evan the tools.

Evan's wearing a t-shirt and jeans, which is equally erotic and irritating. The summer heat is particularly unforgiving this time of year, so why isn't he stripped down to near-nothing yet?

The boys will tell him what I like, I reassure myself. *They'll tell him in small exchanges and secret asides so you won't have to. You can still respect Evan when he's strutting around with his young muscled body bared.* Just the thought stiffens my cock under the warm laptop. At this exact moment, the freckly-faced Stefan has come inside to get something, leaving Evan outside. He passes through the room sporting nothing but a pair of red low-hanging sports shorts, a tease of the crack of his sculpted Irish rump visible. I tell him to come, as if I need something, and when he's close enough, I slip a hand down his front and massage his cock. "Mmm. Just checking it's still there," I assure him playfully, to which his freckly face breaks into a sleepy smile, letting me have my fun.

My lips join in on said fun, too.

The evenings are a bit noisier than usual with the new houseboy. Dinnertime is full of conversation as everyone decides to join, what with our guest that everyone else is interested in and all. I sit in my usual seat at the head of the table while Preston, wearing nothing but a bright blue bikini-brief I bought him, serves us his best cuisine.

Evan, despite his initial shyness, has really clicked with all of the boys. Even Madison, who's usually a bit "off", cracks jokes, asking all about where Evan's from and what he does.

"I want to be a doctor," Evan tells them, to which Jason has a story to contribute about male nurses and how one of his four brothers went into the Army as a medical assistant. Funny, I never knew he had any brothers. Even the man-of-few-words Zac chimes in, saying how his step-dad rigorously pursued becoming a veterinarian before meeting his mom—which I also didn't know. Preston exclaims sleepily that he hates cats, but always wanted a puppy. Madison laughs at that, cheeks full of food.

So many facts I didn't know about my own houseboys. I wonder what else I've let my ears be closed off to over the years, drowned in gold and money and desires. Seems the only thing I've paid attention to were their hot faces, their sculpted bodies, the various fantasies they were unknowingly (and knowingly) lending me.

My dad watches it all, sipping a rum punch from his chair-by-the-pool at Hotel Cloud Nine in his faraway vacation getaway. He watches it all and shakes his head, slurping loudly.

Funny thing about doctors: I have, all my life, despised them. Doctors couldn't help my dad when he collapsed. Don't even properly know what was wrong with him, but my mom said he took a vacation and I believed her. The doctors did whatever doctors do, but it wasn't enough to save me from the life I've now been given. It wasn't enough to save me from my new dad, from Ernest, from the spoils and the glitters of war.

My dad keeps shaking his head, slurping his drink and shaking, shaking, shaking his head.

So useless it seems sometimes, all this medicine and knowledge we have amassed over our long and longer history. All this wisdom, and people still die of paper cuts and bathtubs and sexual appetites.

"I just want to fix people," Evan says in answer to someone's question. "I want to make the world a better place."

All he wants to do is make the world a better place, but after dinner I find Preston chilling out in the living room playing the PS4 all by himself, sprawled out in that skimpy blue bikini, and when our eyes meet, all I want to do is make the world a hornier one. I crawl over Preston's smooth, creamy body. He drops the controller to the ground with a heavy thud, his sharp green eyes piercing me as I climb my bag boy like a lion over prey. He's about to say something witty and cute, but I interrupt him with a hungry, primal kiss, consuming his lips like a second meal.

The new houseboy can try to make the world a better place, sure, as long as I can still surround myself with gorgeous boys and hide among them, and cum among them, and stay horny among them forevermore.

Except for Evan.

The days pass like wads of cum-filled Kleenex, one after the other, enjoyed in its moment, forgotten the next sunrise. I watch as Evan parades about the house conducting his chores in an array of tank tops and ass-hugging shorts. *The clothes are becoming less-so,* I silently note to myself. It's a daily dose of excitement and wake-me-up, really, to eagerly await what adorable outfit he's got planned for the next day. I notice a steady rotation of his clothes when he wears something he's already worn. I've memorized him: his movements, his outfits, his routines. Each morning after my sexy boy Preston makes me one of his tasty omelets, I watch the stairs with growing delight and wait for the beefcake Evan to emerge. I'm paying handsomely for him; I ought to reap whatever joys I can.

Cool your appetites, I warn myself. *You see*

how the others treat you. You see what reputation your loneliness and your horniness and your ... creepiness ... has earned you. I beg myself not to fuck this one up. *Evan is your hardest challenge yet and you are up for it.* Literally "up" for it. Hard. In-my-pants hard.

Maybe I can make the world a better place, too.

[4]

I'm in shock when I poke at a calendar in the study one evening and realize almost a month's already gone by. A month of staring and drooling and hungering. Evan has become best buddies with everyone in the house and I feel like I've hardly had a moment of bonding with him since that limo ride and all-too-short tour of my house. Where's the time gone?

"Zac," I say, drawing his attention from a computer one morning. "Take me to the store." I watch Evan through the window as I talk to Zac, watching Evan's muscles flex and move in his tank top as he rakes the yard.

"*The* store?" Zac quips in his deep, quiet voice. "Any one in particular?"

Where is all this extra attitude coming from? I stare at him, annoyed. "Yes. I pay you to read my mind, don't I? Get the car ready."

"Sorry, boss." He abandons the computer and grabs the keys off the wall.

"Uniform."

He lifts his white-blonde eyebrows at me. "Just for a trip to the store?"

"It's one of the houseboy rules, Zac. You know better than to ask." Why don't the boys just *know*? Evan's just the new houseboy; he isn't some physicalized permission for the others to start slacking. I glare at Evan's sexy figure through the window, filled with a mix of frustration and desire. "Uniform. I'll wait."

"Yes, boss." Zac heads upstairs to don the sorta-required sleeveless white dress shirt and bowtie. I love him in it because he looks like a stripper ready for a show. It's likely a bit humiliating for him to wear, considering we go out in public like that, but a paycheck's a paycheck. He'll wear a blue full-body spandex suit if I so require it. I just might, to punish him for his insolence.

Sulking and staring longingly through the window at that beautiful boy I won't allow myself to have, I wait.

An hour later, I'm browsing aisles of sexy young male clothing with a hard-on. I grip the fabric of one shirt that hangs on the wall, then abandon it for another. I touch the buttons and run a finger along the collars, pinching and rubbing. I imagine pinching and rubbing this collar while it's around the neck of a certain someone. When I brush a hand down the front, I imagine what his abs would feel like through the material. I swallow, hoping the stiffening of my companion downstairs isn't *too* visible.

One of the most frustrating things about buying top-dollar designer clothes is the lack of color choices. The can't-be-bothered haughty fucks in Hollywood or New York or wherever-the-hell decide what colors are "in", then mix and twist their designs to match the season.

While you push through aisles to dress that adorable, muscular eighteen-year-old working in your mansion and stealing all the spotlight, a false sense of choice invades you, deceives you into thinking you're shopping at all when, in fact, all the decisions were already made for you by foofy men and women halfway across the country in some orange sunlit office.

I think all these annoying, pretentious thoughts as I pull a shirt off the rack and hand it to Zac, who stands there less-than-proudly, patiently sweating in his white sleeveless shirt and bowtie. His thick shoulders gleam with a hint of sweat, his biceps shiny. "This one."

Another merciful hour later, I've purchased about thirty-five different items. "Pick yourself out something too," I tell Zac, but he declines, insisting he's got all he needs. Either he means that, or he just wants to get home and *out* of that sexy uniform. *Don't worry, I'll rip that bow off your neck soon enough.* "Of course," I mutter, then pick out a top for him anyway, ensuring it's the right size to fit snug on his thick arms, so really it's a gift for me. *Oh, must every single thing in my life be so sexually motivated?* "Yes," I answer myself out loud, picking out a new, skimpier underwear option for Preston. "Yes, it must." I pull a sexy pair of pants that would make Stefan's stout Irish ass look straight out of a centerfold. *Because what other joys do I have?*

Later when I'm home, I surprise the boys with my gifts. "Look what I got you," I tell Preston in the living room, distracting him from his game. "You too, Madison. Check it out." I watch their reactions as they pull the clothes out of their various shopping bags. I feel tingles up the back of my neck as I watch their soft boyish hands feeling the material, admiring my gifts to them. Preston laughs, then yanks off his shirt right there to try on a new one. It fits tight at the pecs. "You like them?" I ask.

"Thanks!" Preston exclaims, beaming. His bright green eyes meet mine. "What'd I do to earn the new threads?"

"Just being yourself." I give him a wink. "I take care of my boys, right?"

Stefan gives a similar reaction of surprise, happy with what I'd gotten him. Kyle, too. He gives an impressed lift of his eyebrows as he examines the new athletic gear I bought him. "This is pretty legit," he mumbles. "Thanks." His reaction fills my heart up with a cocktail of relief and self-gratification. *The gear is a gift for me, too,* I could say, *on our next training session when I get the pleasure of seeing you in them.*

When I at last find Evan in the backyard, he's by the pool in a chair. "I got you some things," I announce as I awkwardly approach. He gets out of the chair, setting his phone aside, and I watch as his blue eyes light up. I'm a bit relieved to give him his gifts alone and away from the others; I got him considerably more.

"Another?" he says, pulling out the next shirt from the bag. He holds it up to his body, then looks up at me. "A bit small?"

"Just right," I insist. "You like the colors?"

"Love them. Yeah." He gives the last shirt another onceover. Just watching his hands work over the material is so sensual to me, I find myself helplessly entranced. "Thanks a lot, Liam. You really know my style." He chuckles, then tosses the shirts back into the bag. "I feel like I should give you something in return for giving me the best summer job in the world."

"No, no. You give me plenty back with your ... with your hard work." I smile, my eyes drifting to his chest where two perky nipples show through his damp white tee. He must've taken a swim earlier and didn't completely dry off. I have half a mind to tackle him back into the shimmering pool and play a game of water tag. I don't know what the rules are or how to play, but I'm certain it'll end up with one or both of us naked. "I just wanted to ... show you my appreciation."

"I like your appreciation a lot." He gives the shopping bag a squeeze. "By all means, keep appreciating me."

"Oh, I will." The both of us laugh, though I wonder how much *appreciation* he's letting himself see. Has he become aware yet of how many of my promises I've already broken?

Does he even sense my ogling now? Does he think I meant him to pay me back in sexual favors?

Am I just a high schooler again, paying my friends to *be* my friends? Am I trying to buy Evan, just like I bought every single person I've ever known my whole life? Am I just a rich kid paying off the boys on the playground again?

"I got you something else," I tell him, then set a box on the table next to him.

His eyes grow wide as they've ever been, looking down at the white and black box. He doesn't say anything for a moment, overcome.

"It's for college," I explain to him. "You'll need a new one, I'm sure. It's top-notch, has all the bells and *whistling* you might need. Lots and lots of *whistling*."

I smile nervously. Has this gotten his attention? Have I earned his love yet? Will this gift seal the deal, officially making him mine?

Evan looks up from the laptop box, his eyes small and, for the first time, nervous. "I ... I can't ..." He shakes his head. "I can't take this."

"Please. It's on me. College gift. It's my pleasure, please."

"Liam." He looks down at the box again, then shakes his head. "Really, Liam. It's too much. I appreciate it so much but, really, I can't accept this."

I stare at Evan's face, a fear suddenly gripping *my* throat. I've never had one of my gifts rejected before. I've never been told no.

This has never happened.

"I'm sorry," he mutters, red-faced. "I hope I didn't, like, piss you off. I just can't—"

"It's alright." I force myself to smile. "Maybe it's just ... a bit too much, a bit too fast. I'll leave it in your room. You can accept it or ... or just leave it there. It's yours if you want it."

And I apparently can't accept "no" for an answer. I give the box to the laptop a reassuring slap on its surface, pushing that smile at Evan, as if demanding him to be okay, demanding him to go along with what I decree.

"Thanks," he finally says, his wetted eyes downcast.

"Anything else I can get you?" I ask, as if *I'm* the fucking houseboy.

"No. This is great." Evan gives me a little smile, clutching the bag of clothes. "I'm ... I'm gonna get a workout in with Kyle before my shower. I'll catch you later, Liam. Th-Thanks for the, um ..." He lifts the bag, gives me a nod, then heads for the house.

I stay by the pool, paralyzed, and watch through the windows as Evan drops the gift bag into a chair, then heads into the gym where Kyle's wiping down a machine. I don't blink once as I watch a conversation happen between them, words without sound, moving lips, and then they laugh.

Is this all my life's meant to be? All the money in the world and I can't even buy the sweet, male bonding I'm witnessing through the window. Why can't I have that? Why, when I engage in anything sexual with my boys, do I always see that glint of fear in their eyes? It's a glint that asks: *How am I doing?* It asks: *Is this good enough for you?* It asks: *What else do you need me to do so you keep giving me shit and letting me live here and paying for my joys?*

I drop into the lounger that only moments ago cradled Evan's sweet, tight, sultry ass, still watching as the two of them work out together. My arm rests atop the box to the unaccepted laptop, forming sweat. Evan sits at the weight bench while Kyle comes around to spot him. When the set's over, Kyle gives my eighteen-year-old demigod a pat on the back, then they start moving lips again, words, words, words. Just watching them makes me crave one of my chocolate protein bars, which I eat after every punishing workout Kyle puts me through. I wish I knew what the two of them are talking about, but as I witness their chiseled faces break into another bout of laughter, I figure it doesn't matter; the message is clear enough.

Something has to change.

[5]

"What I'm proposing," I tell the boys present when breakfast is served, "is that we take the weekend off."

Preston looks confused. "But who'll feed us if I'm—"

"We'll have food delivered," I answer. "It's all on me. I'm paying. No cleaning. Nothing. I want all of us to take a good solid weekend and just ... kick back and do what we want. How's that sound?" I look to Madison at the end of the bar, who doesn't do much anyway, and he gives a shrug of approval. Jason too, smiling lamely.

Not the enthusiasm I was going for.

"What was that?" It's Kyle who asks the question, padding into the dining area from the front hall, barefoot and wearing nothing but gym shorts.

I die a hundred quick deaths seeing his rippling display of chiseled, perfect muscles.

"Boss is giving us the weekend," Preston tells him, leaning forward on the counter, his biceps popping as he does so. Naturally that goes unmissed, too. I'm juggling what the fuck to look at.

Kyle grunts. "Really?"

I nod, lifting my chin and feeling proud. "Yes. I think it's only fair, with as hard as you all work. So ... no workouts, no training, no protein bar breaks." I smile at him.

"I can spend it with Natalie," he considers.

A stab of annoyance cuts my happiness in half. "Well, yeah," I agree, irritated to say so. I did, after all, just offer them the weekend off. I suppose I had assumed they would be spending their off-time here in my house and bonding with me ... not with some chick across town.

"Dunno what I'll do with my time," says Jason, face scrunched up in thought.

"I imagine you'd use it the same as you use your work time: doing nothing," teases Preston. Jason throws a napkin at him, but it misses and lands by the china cabinet. "Or use it working on your aim, whichever."

"Yeah, good. I'm gonna call Natalie," Kyle decides, turning to head for the stairs.

I glower at his sexy, muscled backside.

Madison and Jason head for the living room after Preston makes some snide remark about kicking their asses in some game I don't even know the name of.

I'm left at the table feeling as empty—or perhaps emptier—than I felt before offering them the weekend off. I was hoping it would've made them ... I don't know. Maybe I wanted a bigger thanks. Maybe buying them all new clothes was a waste, too.

Right on cue, Evan descends from the stairs scantily-dressed in one of the outfits I'd gotten him. *It looks approximately a thousand times better on him than I thought it would.* He drops by the living room first, bypassing me entirely, and I hear some chatter and a laugh or two. They start asking him questions—I can hear it all from the table, the sound of their boyish talk and banter carrying through the wide, empty bowels of the house—and I listen as he gives his advice regarding the game they're playing.

They look to him like a leader. Even after just one month, a confidence has come out of Evan that no interview or background check could find, apparently. The boys ask his advice and look to him for a reaction to everything. Even last week at dinner—it was just five of us, as Zac was driving Kyle to his girlfriend's and Stefan had already eaten—the boys stared at Evan as he shared some medical breakthrough he read about. The boys are in constant awe of him. It doesn't matter the subject; Evan always has something intelligent to contribute to their conversations. Their eyes light up when he speaks and they hang on his every word like golden nuggets of sound.

And I remember that dinner, sitting there with a forkful of peas halfway to my mouth, staring as the boys listened to Evan, transfixed in their own way. Evan had them in his palm.

Has them in his palm.

In the shower, I'm furious with myself and I don't know why. All the shampoos in the world can't cleanse my hair or mind of all the dirtiness in it. All the hundreds of dollars of soaps and body washes and fragrances can't wash away the foul stench of my selfishness.

There's no boys here. There won't be any boys in my bed. Everyone is staring at Evan all day long and I brought this on myself.

I grab my limp cock and jerk it.

Evan and his cute, cocky smirk. Evan and his bright eyes and dark hair and infinite depth. Evan and his super interesting backstory and those little ears of his and that stupid button nose. Evan and his eighteen years of charm.

I jerk and jerk and jerk.

Where did I go wrong? I just wanted a new toy, that's what it is. I wanted someone else in the house—like Kyle, like Preston, like Jason, like Madison, like Zac, like Stefan—that would spend all their time convincing me that I'm not just a needy, pervy, spoiled rich boy loser.

I shut my eyes, press my face to the shower wall, and jerk and jerk and jerk.

I am so insecure that I need to pile beautiful boys into my home to convince me that I'm worth something. I want my mounds and heaps of gold and dollars and self-entitlement to mean more than zeroes in a computer somewhere.

I want my dad at his seaside condo in Heaven to stop watching me so judgmentally while sipping from his hollowed-out coconut drinks with the umbrella in them.

I look down and I'm still soft as a worm. I can't even cry about it anymore. See, there's this expensive cream I bought, and I've been putting it on my face for a decade now, and I think it's somehow damaged me, left me unable to cry. The money took away all my tears. Took away all the fucks I could be giving. Took away my cleverness.

Gave me Evan.

Evan and his stupid, perfect self.

When the sun's set and Kyle's taken off to spend the weekend with his female lady-friend and the boys are in the living room still playing that fucking game, I crawl down the stairs like some overdone lobster and stand in the hall hugging a robe to my wet body. I stare at the boys in the living room, listening to Evan and Jason tease each other, listening to Madison howl when his guy gets blown up. I don't interrupt. I don't ask them to fuck each other while I jerk off. I don't ask Stefan to put on music and dance like Oliver used to ... the last boy I tossed out like trash. "Well done," Preston keeps saying, admiring Evan's keen game-playing. He throws an arm over the back of the couch, brings it around Evan's shoulder and gives him a squeeze.

You get whatever it is you want, Preston told me once. *Just snap your fingers and it's yours.* Yes, I can get whatever it is I want. But the more I reach for it, the more it seems to pull away.

The more I take, the less I seem to have.

[6]

I take a place at the bar, swiveling in my stool like a bored kid and counting the seconds before sexy, strutting Preston comes around the corner. "You need something, boss?"

"Isn't this your weekend off?" I ask lamely.

"It is," he agrees, as if I had just reminded him. "Guess I'm eager to feed you something." He laughs, finding himself funny.

He's wearing a white sleeveless button shirt, opened and floating in the air as he moves across the kitchen. His pale blue jeans hang just low enough to show a tease of his underwear. *He's wearing the skimpy new ones you bought him,* I tell myself, encouraged. "So what's your taste this fine day?" He swings open the fridge.

"You."

He looks up suddenly, his cute eyebrows pulling together. "Ooh," he says, his silky voice changing. "I see, I see. Well, I gotta warn you, I just woke up and ... haven't had a chance to shower. After all, my *amazing boss* gave me the weekend off, so I've been a bit ..." He considers the word, then finishes, "lazy."

"'Amazing', you said?"

"Amazing. And, well, I know the number one houseboy rule is to stay clean for the boss, and you *do* like your boys super clean, so I'm feeling a bit—"

"I like my boys however they come," I tell him, which isn't exactly true, but I'm not going for honesty; I'm going for desperately-in-need-of-someone's-undivided-attention. "Hey, I was thinking maybe we'd retry that fudge lesson one of these days. You know the one ... the lesson in fudge-making that we never quite got around to completing."

He studies my face, perhaps to judge whether I'm being sincere. "Got a bit messy last time, if I recall, didn't it?"

"Quite."

He closes the fridge softly, figuring my appetite isn't so much for food, and saunters across the kitchen. Meeting me at the bar, he leans into it, lifting his eyes to meet mine. "I'm thinking maybe you're not *really* so much in the mood for chocolate. Am I right?" I shrug coyly. "Perhaps you feel more ... hot and spicy?"

When I grin, he knows he's got me. Preston stands back, then slowly starts to tease his shirt off his body. I watch with thrill, with mounting impatience, with a satisfied smirk as he slowly unveils his creamy, smooth body. He turns it into a dance, hopping to some imaginary beat. One side of the shirt slips off, then the other, and he slowly, slowly, slowly wiggles it down his arms, moving to our imaginary striptease song. I even start to move my shoulders, a grin spreading across my face as I hungrily watch.

Preston's an expert at serving a meal.

He pops the button on his jeans, holding his pose there for a bit while I appreciate the fitness model-caliber upper torso he so casually sports. His arms are flexed in his jean-button-gripping pose where I see veins that trace down his biceps and forearms, even down his hands. His roguishly-curved eyebrows play with me, his bright eyes watching me watch him. He knows I want it. He's so good at this. I'm no Evan, but in this moment, I'm all Preston cares about.

"Enjoying the show?" he asks, gripping the zipper now. His arms move deliciously, thick and taut. I have a sudden urge to lick them like two dripping mounds of peach ice cream. "Want to put your hands on them?"

It's always what I want. It's always my decision. It's always a hot boy in front of me slowly trying to please me, hoping not to make a wrong move, hoping not to dissatisfy me.

Why can't I just enjoy the show and not be, at all times, hyper aware of the "service" of these boys to me? What the fuck keeps holding me back from just ... letting go?

"Yes," I say, ignoring my thoughts. "I want to put my hands and my tongue all over your mounds of peaches and cream."

He snorts, a laugh, and the character he's put on is thrown by my corny-as-fuck remark.

"Something funny?" I ask.

A flicker of worry crosses his face, and then he recovers, resuming his seduction act right away. "Not at all, boss."

He gives me a wink, as if to reassure me that everything's totally okay. Everything is totally not okay.

"Come here, boss. Put your hands all over my peaches and cream." He lifts an arm to tempt me, giving the bicep a little pop.

I come around the bar counter, draw myself up to his body. He's taken aback by how close I come, startled, and I push him into the counter. The aggression clearly comes unexpectedly, as another look of surprise takes Preston's face, but I ignore it and plunge my face into his chest. He gasps when I latch my mouth onto his muscular pec and grapple his hips with my hungry hands. I act with such ferocity, he might think I were trying to suck his heart out of his nipple.

Fuck. Maybe I am.

Quite suddenly, I grab his wrists and thrust them above his head, pinning them to the doors of the cabinet above. My tongue traces up the line of his pec until my face is buried in his armpit. Smooth as silk, he's even shaved there. *I like my boys clean.* He smells remarkably fresh, considering his comment about not showering.

"You smell great," I decide to let him know, speaking with my lips buried in his pit. Preston only chuckles—amused, I guess—and I pull away to pay witness to his drunken, lazy expression. "I want to taste-test every inch of you for breakfast."

"Careful. Wanna make sure to leave some of me for lunch, dinner, and a midnight snack."

I grip his jeans and pull them down with a force that threatens to tear them. He gasps again, his eyes darting left and right, as if in fear that one of the other guys will oversee this.

Really? I want to say. *After seventeen months of knowing what I'm like, you want to pick now to be self-conscious?* I pull on the waistband to his briefs and slowly slip them down.

"Going there, are we?" he says from high above. "I didn't know you—Oh, fuck."

He's rendered silent because my lips just wrapped around his cock. It was only at a semi, but as my lips and tongue twist around it like an expert masseuse, I feel him swelling and swelling and swelling in my mouth.

"You aren't—You don't—" He keeps trying to speak, keeps changing his mind on what to say. He already sounds out of breath. I *love* that I'm doing this to him. "You've never gone down on—on—"

I pull off his cock, wipe my mouth with a finger, then reply, "I get what I want."

"Keep getting it then," he begs me.

His cock goes back in and I feel him moan through his body. My hands reach up, tickling down his rolling hills of abs, sliding down his smooth as silk hips, his thighs. Every push and pull of my mouth, I feel his cock respond with a pulsing throb. I take that to be his approval of how crazy I'm driving him.

He grabs my hair ... then lets go.

I look up, pulling my mouth off his swollen member to say, "Why'd you let go? Grab it if you want."

"I didn't know if I could—I didn't know if—"

Questioning. Worrying. Touching me like I'm glass. I can't stand these extra sensitivities. "Grab my hair, Pres. Grab it hard."

He does, but gently. He might as well be petting me. I guess that'll do. I bring myself back to sucking his cock.

What's missing?

When I come up from the finished job to meet his eyes, he lifts his eyebrows, out of breath, and says, "That was amazing. I don't know what I did to earn that, but—"

"Just being you," I say, smiling. "Just you remember this next time I tell you how much I appreciate you. You're my best boy." I give

Preston a caress of my hand at the side of his head. I am a sexual monster. I'm a hundred law suits begging to be filed. I am a boy-parasite. "I wanted you. And I have you. And I'm lucky."

"And Liam Hightower always gets what he wants," Preston finishes for me, smiling.

Staring into his eyes, I hear his words over and over and over. I hear his words and I wonder why I still feel like I don't have anything I want. I hear his words and I hear the dumb ones I just uttered to him.

He seems to have heard them too. "Best boy, huh?" he says back, chuckling lightly. "Funny. I kinda got the impression that Evan was your best boy."

I frown. "He's my *newest*," I affirm, "but yet to be determined if he's my best."

"Considering how well he's picked up everything," Preston reasons, "I'd say he's the best you've hired. He's quick. He's smart. He's also really clever and the other guys kinda look up to him. It's weird, isn't it? Considering how young he is and everything." His face twists in thought, his lips pouting, eyes curious. "Don't you think so?"

I hear his words. I know what he means. I can't deny the impression Evan's made.

I need to change the life I have, to figure out the life I want. I'm sick of being sick of myself. I want to be proud of the monster I've become and bear to look at myself for longer than ten seconds in a mirror. I want to be their leader, the guy they respect, their anchor ... but it's Evan who's their leader, it's Evan who they respect, it's Evan who's their anchor.

"Yes," I finally agree, inspiration dawning in my eyes. "The new houseboy is ... amazing."

Preston gives me a little kiss on the cheek, then leaves me there in the kitchen to dance with all the thoughts, both dark and inspiring, that have just been born.

[7]

When sunlight no longer burns through the windows, I pass up the curved stair and knock on Evan's door. Minutes pass before he finally answers my third knock. He wears a loose-fitting tank that threatens to show his nipples and a pair of gym shorts. His hair is wet and his blue eyes sparkle.

It's been a long time since I've stood so close to him, I'd almost forgotten the effect his simple presence has on me. "Evan," I say for a greeting. "I brought you a bonus paycheck."

"Bonus?" His eyes light up as he takes the envelope from my hand. With expert fingers, he runs a nail along the edge and extracts the papers. "Wow," he says, clearly surprised. "I didn't know we were getting bonuses."

"I'm only giving one to *you*," I tell him, quiet as a secret. He meets my eyes. "You've made a big impression. Clearly, you've gone above and beyond what was expected of you and … you're excelling in all of your work," I admit, flattering him to the point of blushing.

I hope the flattery carries long enough to embrace what else I'm about to ask of him.

"Thanks, Liam," he says. Hearing him say my name makes me surge with pleasure. Most of the boys call me "boss", whether sincerely or tongue-in-cheek, but Evan is the only one who consistently uses my first name. "This really means a lot to me. I wish there was more I could do. My job really isn't difficult at all."

"I do have something in mind," I let slip, staring down at his chest while I speak. I can't quite meet the intensity of his beautiful blue eyes, not with what I'm about to ask. "A way I think you could help me."

"Yeah?"

I stall, drawing myself into his room and running a finger along the headboard. I imagine what he looks like when he sleeps. Does he sleep in his underwear? Does he wear anything to bed at all? "I'm sorry I deceived you in the limo ride, Evan."

I'm not looking at him, so I can't judge his reaction. All I get is silence for a short spell. I hear him shift his feet.

Let's elaborate. "I told you that I wouldn't expect sex. I told you it's not a part of the deal, but ... but clearly I need that." I lift my face, but still can't meet his eyes. "I'm lonely."

"You're paying me a bonus to have sex with you?"

He puts it so bluntly, I suddenly find my tongue to have been swallowed. "No," I finally manage to say. "No, no. I'm ... What I meant was that I ... I'm just saying I'd—"

"The boys feel used."

Now I look at him, startled by this new information. "W-What do you mean?"

"You make them wear things," he says. "You make them do things. You make them have sex with you and … and with each other. I've heard it all. Your houseboy rules. I saw it once when you didn't even know I was there. I saw you jerking while Jason and Madison—" Evan cuts himself off. The look in his blue eyes crushes me … a look of disdain.

How long has he known? Are all the boys speaking such poison about me? Even Jason and Madison? Even … Even Preston?

"This is who I am," I finally say, unable to defend any of it. "This is your boss. This is Liam. I'm horny and very lonely and *horribly* unhappy and I surround myself with beautiful boys to make it all better. You're one of them, even though I've never put a hand on you."

"But you *want* to put a hand on me," Evan says, as if to be sure. "That's why you're giving me this?" He waves the bonus check in the air.

"Of *course* I do. Evan, you're beautiful."

He frowns at that. The flattery doesn't touch him. "Why are you so unhappy?"

I can't possibly put it into words. Already, my resolve has crumbled. Whatever I was hoping to accomplish with that stupid bonus, it's failed miserably. I drop onto the bed at my side—onto his bed—and I shake my head, unable to produce an answer.

Evan's face wrinkles, concentrating. His eyes wander, bright blue and crystalline, and his lips pout while he seems to consider my wordlessness.

The longer the silence persists, the worse my heart races. *I could lose him,* I realize. I feel so dizzy. My chest is a cage of riled up bees.

"I think," Evan says finally, "that you want me to help you. To *truly* help you. And that's why you've paid me. I think we need to have ourselves a little ... experiment."

Now it's my turn to look confused. I stare at him, uncomprehending.

"You've been very used to getting what you want, right?" Evan asks, as if reading my mind. I simply nod, wide-eyed and slack-jawed. "I think it's time you get a little taste of your own home-cooked fudge." His blunt black eyebrows pull together tauntingly, all his wet spiky hair seeming to move too. Even his little ears flinch cutely. "I think it's time for a little ... change of the rules."

"What k-kind of change?" I blurt out, my breath quickening.

"I think this 'bonus' of yours needs to be a promotion." Evan nods, certain of his idea now, even though I still haven't the faintest what this idea of his is. "You're gonna make me head houseboy. I want to be in charge of the others, and *not* you."

My eyes screwed intently to his, I'm buried in sudden thoughts. "I ... don't think I follow."

"I'm gonna treat you like you're *my* boy. I'm going to be the new boss. Put you beneath me. Don't let you have what you want. Deprive you of all your sweet luxuries you love so much, including *us*. I'll make you my ... pet."

Just hearing the words, my eyes disconnect from his, drifting down to his tight, chiseled chest in that tank top ... right where a nipple's snuck out the side. A wave of undeserved pleasure seizes me. I've never been so turned on by an idea. I've never had a boy *tell* me what it's going to be like. I'm hearing Evan's words. He isn't asking my permission. He's just telling me how it's going to be.

"Okay," I finally say, like my mind's still catching up, wrapping around the depraved, overwhelming concept of what he's suggesting. "You ... *want* to do this?"

"I already am," he says, arms folded.

"But ... But the other boys ...?"

"They'll *love* it." The smug smirk on his face is a strange and terrifying combination of cute-as-fuck and menacing. "You see how I am with them," he says, lifting a challenging brow. "I exude confidence. I take charge. The other boys listen to me."

My heart thrusts and thrusts, trying to break free from the prison of my ever-confining ribcage. Evan puts a hand to his thigh, starts to rub, starts to tap a rhythm. His head bobs to a tune in his head—that thing he does when he thinks and thinks and thinks. Already I see wicked plots and ideas swimming through his head as he waits for my response.

"You're ready to play boss, Evan?"

The tapping of his thigh goes on and on, a beat of thoughts, a drumming of pros and cons and in-betweens ... and then at once the song ends. His wild blue eyes meet my own. When the look of victory washes over his adorable face and a smug curl becomes of his full lips, I know his answer.

That smug look on his face, that's the most dangerous look of all.

[8]

Sunday pours a wash of light on my face as I wake on the last day of freedom for my boys. When I stretch and come to notice the sheets tenting with my steel-hard morning wood, I'm suddenly reminded of my exchange with Evan. I rub my eyes, swim out of my bed sheets and stare at the mirror across the room. I wonder if I expected myself to look different.

As if some agreement with a boy would change my world and right all my wrongs.

"You're a fool, Liam Hightower," I say to that reflection across the room. "You're a fool, and a horny fool at that, and no more."

I descend the stairs lazily in just a white tee and my silky pajama pants. Padding across the white tile foyer, I come to the kitchen and open the fridge, curious what's for breakfast. Pulling a hard-boiled egg, a slice of cheese and a glass of orange juice to the counter, I start tapping the egg, and only now realize that I haven't cracked open my own hard-boiled egg in probably a decade. The shell comes off so stubbornly, it's like picking shards of glass off a ball of glue. By the time I strip it of its shell, I've mutilated it beyond a recognizable shape. Eating the sad thing, I find tiny pieces I neglected to see, picking them out of my teeth. *Haven't seen Evan yet*, I tell myself, *and I've already managed to deprive myself of a decent breakfast.*

Sipping on my glass of orange juice, I bring it to the living room, only to find it empty. Interesting. I move to the stairs, but hear no activity. Then I make for the back windows.

That's when I see him. Standing by the pool, Evan's chatting with Jason, Madison, Stefan and Preston. That's everyone except for

Kyle, who's at his girlfriend's, and Zac, who is likely still asleep. I can't tell what Evan's saying, but whatever it is, he has the other boys' undivided attention.

Instantly, my mouth goes dry as a wind tunnel and I can't breathe. I stare out the window, watching them with unblinking eyes. A cold, bony hand clutches my chest and locks up my central nervous system. I can't even bring my glass of juice to my lips, paralyzed as I am.

Then, on cue, Evan turns, looking back at the window, noticing me. The other boys do too, all their eyes finding mine.

Rigid as a statue attempting to come to life, I give them a subtle nod of acknowledgement, then turn and direct myself back to the kitchen. I can't even say if I nodded at all with how stiff my body's been rendered by fear. For all I know, they just watched me stand there like a staring ghoul, then stalk off. I shuffle around the kitchen, pacing, then finally settle myself at the bar and clench what remains of my glass of juice like it were a lifeline. I nurse it, kissing the glass but not really sipping; I can't trust myself not to choke.

Too soon, I hear the opening and closing of the back door. I can't tell which of the boys has come in, but only one pair of footsteps crosses the tiles. I listen to them—click, clack, click, clack—and then they approach the kitchen bar where I'm seated.

I look up. Evan stands there in a tight new shirt I bought him—a deep blue color to match his eyes with an off-center white stripe down the side. His tight jeans, bunched up at his white shoes, make a show of his crotch where I notice he's wearing a white leather belt. It's difficult to dare my eyes any farther up than his pecs, which are perfectly hugged by that shirt as if it were tailored for him.

When my eyes meet his, the world quakes and I lose all my resolve. His face is steeled, his jaw locked, and his eyes burrowing into me. There is no mistaking it: Evan is the head boy in charge, and he knows it.

"Liam," he says.

I can't produce a single word at first. Then, after setting down my glass, I dare to lift my chin to the head boy in charge and softly reply: "Good morning, Evan."

"I've made a few decisions," he tells me.

I swallow hard. I try to lick my lips, but there's nothing to lick them with; my tongue's somehow paralyzed and my mouth is still dry. "Decisions?" I finally say, though it comes out in a rasp.

"Yep." He tilts his head, allowing me the pleasure of witnessing the smug smirk that's taken his flushed, boyish face. "The boys and I have decided on a few new ... *house rules.*"

I feel my breathing's changed. I feel my heart speeding up. I feel myself wanting to hear him, but all the learned logics and comforts in my mind war against my bodily reaction. Those logics tell me he isn't serious. Those logics tell me there's no way I can truly submit to him. I can't play the role of "submissive boy" in my own house. I can't take it seriously.

"New rule," he says. "No kisses. No feels. No touching. We decide when you touch us. We decide when you kiss us. We decide when you put your hands on our bodies." His voice is soft and silky as always, yet somehow stern. I get the immediate impression that none of his "rules" are up for negotiation.

Unwilling to grovel at his feet just yet, I simply clasp my hands and nod once.

"I want to repeat myself so you understand. *I* decide what you get to kiss or touch from now on." He waits for me to acknowledge his words; I do so with another subtle nod. "You don't put your hands on any of the boys without my permission. You put me in charge, I'm going to be in charge. I run this house. I'm the new boss. You're the new houseboy."

His words ring in my ears with the sound of finality. I fight an inappropriate urge to chuckle, laugh him off, giggle and tell him I change my mind and I'll take the bonus back. But something deep and scary within me says it's far, far too late to change my mind.

"I'm going to need to pick up some things. When Zac wakes up, he'll take me where I need to go. I'll need your card."

I frown. "My card? I just paid you last night."

"Oh?" Evan's soft face crushes into a laugh, his lips spreading to show white teeth against his flushed, boyish face. "Oh, no, houseboy. I'm not using *my* hard-earned money."

I gape at Evan. Is he serious? "I'm—Well, I have to, uh ... Preston uses the house card to—"

"Get the groceries? Alright. That makes all this easier." Another smug smirk crosses his sweet face; I never expected him to be capable of such dominance ... such unwavering power. "When I'm gone, I want you to pack my clothes for me and put them into a nice suitcase. Make it pretty. Treat my clothes like gold—I don't want any of them wrinkled."

Fear lances through me. "Y-You're moving out?"

At that, he laughs. "Chill, houseboy. No one's moving out of this house, least of all me.

I'm just getting ... settled in," he finishes, his teeth flashing brightly. "Remember, houseboy, no wrinkles. We'll be back for dinner."

"*We* ... ?"

"Yes, we. The boys are coming with me. We're gonna have a day on the town ... at your expense. Oh, and dinner's your responsibility too. You're cooking for us, since Preston's got the weekend off. I'll expect dinner at seven."

"Dinner," I repeat, like it's some strange word I've never heard before.

"Don't let me down on your first day as the new houseboy," Evan says, his eyebrows lifting like a warning. "I'd hate for you to earn some awful punishment on your very first day."

I swallow hard. "Ev—Evan ..."

"Don't let me down, houseboy."

With that, he turns and heads for the stairs to fetch Zac. The momentary glimpse of his backside in those sexy clothes I bought him makes my insides crawl with horniness. I'm left there in the kitchen, stupefied, rendered dumb and numb.

It seems like seconds later that Evan comes down the stairs ... and all the boys are trailing behind him. Stefan's nervous eyes meet mine. Madison's dull ones. Jason's puppy eyes. Even Preston glances at me, his green eyes full of youth and playfulness and light. Tall and stoic Zac pushes forward, keys swinging at his long fingertips as he aims for the door.

"We'll be back by seven," Evan repeats, speaking on behalf of all the boys, apparently. "We'll be hungry. Let's go, boys."

The whole crew heads for the door. For half an insane second, I'm actually convinced that they're all abandoning me. I'm convinced that my stupid idea has suddenly talked the boys out of working for me at all. They all think I'm some weird perverted fucker and this is their grand escape. After months and years of service, they're leaving.

"Guys," I say to their backs as they move across the foyer. "Guys, seriously?" None of them look in my direction. They're all playing their parts perfectly. "Guys ...?"

The door shuts behind them and the silence that takes grip of the house afterward is cold and unforgiving. I move to the front window and watch as they pile into *my* limo. I watch as they throw arms around each other's backs, laughing, led on by Evan and his cocky, flushed and adorable face. I hear their muted laughter through the glass before the doors to the limo cut off all sound.

Then they're gone. I stand at the glass. My mouth hangs open. My stomach falls through the floor.

And it is not lost on me the raging erection in my silken pants.

[9]

First thing I do after they leave is go to their bedrooms and confirm that their personal belongings are still there. They are. *No, stupid, they didn't just up and leave you.* My insecurities emerge, telling me to fear every little bit of this experience I'm having. My insecurities want not to trust an ounce of it.

My erection says: bring it on.

I calm my nerves by taking an afternoon shower. With the house to myself, I feel eerily vulnerable. No one's downstairs. The boys are out and, legitimately, could return at any time. I find myself checking the bathroom door five times after getting naked and running the water. Then, paranoia enslaving my brain, I opt to lock the door—both bedroom *and* bathroom—and commence in taking my shower safely. I let the warm water run down my body and, with an amused chuckle, I wonder if I'm *allowed* to be taking this shower.

Suddenly, I find myself turned on by the fantasy of Evan owning me. I *allow* myself to be turned on by it. *Maybe you'll get what you paid for all along, after all.* I let my cock be rock-hard even as the water and soap and gels run down it teasingly, slick and slippery. I don't jerk off. Erections, in my recent past, have become something of a golden commodity.

The *reality* of Evan owning me, however, is a bit humiliating. I can't stand not knowing what the other boys think of it all. Are they getting a sick thrill out of it? Or is it a joke to them? Have I, all this time, been some dumb rich idiot they've been taking advantage of? Maybe none of them really respect me. Maybe they were all waiting for this chance to put me down, to put me where I belong, to deny me the pleasures I've been so greedily taking since the day I brought each of them into my home.

Just like the kid at recess who paid off the bullies who almost gave him two black eyes. Just like the cocky high schooler who bought his prom date, who bought the prom king, who bought the respect of the football team. Just like the college fool who bought his good grades and paid for his friends' meals and the booze at their parties. Maybe, of all that respect I thought I was purchasing, I actually attained none. Maybe, in fact, I'd never gained any respect at all. *Look at that fool and his money*, they probably said behind my back. *That rich, entitled kid with the big fancy cars and the huge house and the shiny shoes.*

I hear my dad's laughter, even from so far away, echoing from a bathroom stall in the tropical resort in Heaven where he stays. He's reading Heaven's newspaper while sitting on the Great Pot In The Sky and he's laughing his ass off, laughing at his poor, sad son.

After I dry off, I check the clock and note that it's already fifteen past two. I sit at my computer, figuring I have plenty of time before they're back, and browse the web tiredly. I already feel worn out from all the sexual and emotional stimulation I've had since last night.

So many boys. So many desires. I clench shut my eyes, annoyed that, for as long as I've known these boys, I sometimes fear I don't know them at all.

That's when I get the clever idea to open my credit card account. When the list of recent charges appear on the screen, I gape. I'm pretty sure I'm reading it wrong, so I lean into the screen and widen my eyes. Two thousand in a clothing store. Nine hundred dollars in another. One thousand and seventy at a hardware store. Each pending charge, my cock pulses, getting harder and harder. Each charge, I imagine Evan's hand squeezing my cock tighter.

This is real. This is happening.

This is what you asked for, I have to remind myself. *He is doing precisely what you told him to do.* Except I didn't expect him to carry on with the role so ... thoroughly.

I go to his room and, fetching the finest suitcase I can find from the closet, I slowly open his drawers and withdraw his clothes piece by piece. This experience becomes very sexual for me, especially when I get to his underwear. I resist every creepy, obsessive urge to bury my face in them. One by one, I fold and pack them into the suitcase. *Why the fuck does he need me to pack his clothes?* I keep asking myself. *What the fuck does he have up his sleeves?* I pack his jeans, imagining how many times they've touched his firm, sculpted ass ... and how many times I *haven't*. I pack his shirts and imagine the perfect bod he's been hiding in those clothes of his. Even with the number of times he's jumped in my pool, I've never dared to go out back with him to watch. I've held him in my mind as something sacred, a person I needed to preserve and protect—even from myself— someone I had to respect, above all else. I wanted to do this right.

The suitcase packed, all I have left to take care of is dinner, if I'm right. Seeing as I'm utterly incapable of cooking, I call a place that's catered dinner for my household before. On the phone, I'm suddenly transformed back into my old self: master of the house, head man in charge, the boss. The man on the other end of the line knows me and I put in my order for a perfect dinner for the boys. Just hearing the menu options on the phone makes me salivate. Between the incoming gourmet dinner and the fact that I haven't eaten a speck of anything since that sad excuse for a breakfast, I'm reeling with dizziness.

I drop into the couch in the living room and shut my eyes, dreaming of Evan and waiting for time to carry me swiftly into the evening.

Instead, it carries me tortuously slow. Unable to find *any* rest within me, I toss and turn on the couch, frustrated and impatient and horny. How can he stay out so fucking long, hopping around town and spending *my* money? The thought, which had originally intoxicated me with sexual yearning, now fills me with indignance. I have apparently spent nearly four thousand dollars today and haven't even stepped foot outside my house. All those stores know my boys; they're approving the sales. I send them on errands all the time. The store clerks know me by name and wouldn't question a single transaction. The boys could buy every color selection in every store. They could buy a yacht. They could buy a helicopter. They could buy an igloo.

Money can buy many things, but it can't buy seven o'clock getting here any faster.

When the doorbell rings at half past six, I'm elated. Rushing to the door in a button shirt and jeans, I let in the delivery. Directing them with my expected micromanagement finesse, I have them set all the food up on the long dining room table, the various fancily-covered dishes presented on hot plates to keep them warm. You couldn't find a better-looking dinner table in the city. I pay the caterers handsomely and tip them extra to hurry off my property before the boys return. Then, after the door shuts, I cross my arms and wait. The delicious scent of herbed pork bellies, creamy pastas, braised veal, steamed vegetables, and candied potatoes teases my nostrils and drives me near to insanity.

Right on time, the limo pulls up at seven. I watch anxiously through the window as the boys step out of the limo. To my surprise, none of them are carrying anything. Where'd all their purchases go? Evan leads the group, all of them laughing and bantering as they approach the door. They've clearly had a fun-filled day at my expense, just as planned.

The door opens and the noise of their frivolity explodes obnoxiously into the foyer, disturbing the silence that had so arrested this house all day. "Greetings, boys," I tell them. "How was your—?"

"Our stuff's in the car," Evan says, cutting me off. "Will you bring it all in for us?"

"Your ... Your stuff?"

"Yes. Wow, dinner smells great." Evan turns to the boys. "Hope you boys are hungry.

Dinner's waiting." Brushing past me like I were a fencepost, the boys follow him toward the dining room where the delicious feast awaits them. One of them—I don't turn in time to see who—swats my ass on his way past me. "Don't forget to bring in our stuff, houseboy," Evan calls back at me, his voice echoing across the foyer, echoing off the tiles and giving his voice the effect like it's the house itself ordering me.

I'm starving, weak and irritable, and he's making me go out to the limo to bring in their things. My first instinct is to yell at him and throw something, but I neither have a thing readily available to throw, nor do I have an ounce of strength to yell. So, I succumb and push out the door, making for the limo in my front driveway. Upon opening its door, I find the long car filled with bags upon bags upon bags of who-the-fuck-knows.

Why is this turning me on so much? The act of being ordered around by my sexy boys, Evan in charge of them? Staring at the bags, I grow harder and harder. *I'm their bitch.*

It takes me twenty-two minutes to bring in all of the bags. I have to make multiple trips because the bags are so big, I can hardly carry more than two at a time. My eyes skim the top of the bags, curious what all they've purchased with *my* money, but somehow not daring to actually snoop inside them. *I must respect the boys. I'm not allowed to look.* Just thinking that makes me even harder.

Not to mention, none of the bags are particularly forgiving in weight. When I bring the last one in, I'm dragging and my arms tremble the way they do after one of my worst workout sessions with Kyle. *It's almost like Kyle's doing this to me, working me out beyond exhaustion, punishing me, making me suffer.*

Each movement of my legs, each step, my already-hard cock is grazed, made harder.

Horniness: nature's best medicine.

Sweating, exhausted, spent as my wallet likely is, I finally meet the boys in the dining room. All the dishes have been opened and picked through generously by the six hungry houseboys. The aroma of a steaming gourmet feast enters my nostrils like a welcomed friend.

That's when I notice Evan in my seat. *My seat*, at the head of the table. As if just now noticing me, he stops chewing and lifts his chin. "Did you bring in our things?" he asks.

Just the way he asks sends a sharp jolt of sexual hunger through me. *I am his pet.* My eyes scan the other boys warily, suddenly finding myself self-conscious. To my surprise, they're eating casually and seem not to notice that I've become their lowly footman in the space of a single day. They fill their cheeks with the succulent food I brought and had delivered for them. The gamers Madison and Jason carry on some side conversation while the green-eyed Preston asks freckly Stefan to pass the sweet rolls. They're all carrying on as if nothing's strange or different about today. For a moment, I could believe that I've been their slaving houseboy already for a month.

But it's only been a day. "Yes," I tell Evan. "I brought the bags in."

"And where'd you put them?" he asks, stuffing his mouth with a steaming forkful of honey-glazed chicken that could make a hungry man cry. I could cry. I could fucking cry.

"In the foyer by the stairs."

"Nope. Lazy."

Those two words cut into me, my cock so hard it could explode through my pants. I want to whip it out and jerk off right here. I've never been more turned on in my life.

Evan has more to say. "You need to take our things to the upstairs game room." He explains this to me in a very condescending, should-have-known-that-already sort of way, like I'm the house idiot. "Finish your work, then hurry back. Your food's gonna get cold."

I gawp, helplessly leaking in my pants from this treatment. *Your food's gonna get cold??*

"Better hurry," he advises. "I'm sure you're starving, especially with all this delicious grub you got us. Hey, boys ... you liking the grub?"

"Tastes great," admits the cheeky Stefan, his big mouth full of potato.

"Delish," chimes in Preston. "But maybe because it's someone else's cooking and not my own, for once." He grins, his green eyes flashing, and nudges Jason with an elbow, who nods quietly in agreement.

Ignoring their further quips and remarks, I turn and make for the piles of bags I'd left at the foot of the stairs. I take in one long breath, then exhale. The trip from the limo was long. The trip from here to the upstairs game room will be longer.

That fact alone could make me cum hard.

I should've snuck a bite before they came in. I feel awfully, horribly stupid now. Even with as hungry and irritable as I am, my cock is swelling like a restless, desperate friend.

Bright side: I'm sporting more wood today than I have in months.

Thirty-eight minutes pass before I bring the last bag to the game room. Entirely wasted beyond seeing straight, I stagger back down the stairs and slump sulkily across the white tile to the dining room.

The serving plates are gone. The table is a mess of napkins, dirty plates, and half-empty glasses. There's a stain of gravy running across my beautiful tablecloth. Crumbs dust the chairs and floor.

Seated at the head of the table, Evan still remains. The sole occupant. A fork in his hand, an empty plate in front of him, he seems to have been waiting for me. When my tired eyes meet his striking, happy blue ones, my chest fills with anticipation.

"Bags put up?"

"Yes," I answer numbly.

"Good. Dinnertime then, huh?"

"Yes." I lick my lips, turn to study the table, confused where all the food's gone. "But where's the—"

"Oh! You thought—?" Evan chuckles, so amused by something I'm clearly missing. "No, houseboy. That was *our* meal."

I gape. "But ... But I had it delivered and ... and I had it catered for ... for ..."

"And we loved every bite of it."

I can't produce a single word for a minute, staring blankly at Evan's smug, adorable face. "You can't possibly have eaten *all* that food. I ordered enough for all of us twofold."

"Preston packed up the rest and stored it in the fridge. We'll eat it tomorrow if we feel like it." He grins, kicking back in his chair and throwing his hands behind his head.

"Then ... what am *I* going to eat?"

"I picked you up a little something on the way home," he answers, his voice light and casual. "Kyle told me something you like."

At that, he rises from his chair, then reaches back. He struggles, his face scrunched up as he tediously works something out of his rear pocket. When it's freed, he holds the thing in his palm. For a moment I can't even identify what the fuck it is.

Then I realize it's a protein bar.

"Put it in my pocket," he says, wincing, "then forgot about it. You said something about liking these? They remind you of Kyle's tough workouts? Been sitting on it for an hour or two now." He wiggles his palm, the sad protein bar sitting in it, squashed, misshapen, crinkling in its sad white wrapper. "Probably a bit warm. My ass warmed it up for you, I guess."

I look at him with such scathing insolence, it's a wonder his face doesn't burn off. But that adorable face remains intact, unaffected, smug and certain, and that sat-on protein bar—my dinner, apparently—awaits.

"You gonna thank me?" he asks, as if *he's* the one that ought to be offended.

I'm so hungry my arms shake. I can hardly lift them from my sides to mind an itch at my ear, or a sore spot at my shoulder. I just stare at Evan and feel my stomach groan with neglect.

"Thank you," I finally say. I take six steps, then reach for the protein bar.

"No, no," he says. "Allow me. I insist."

He slowly tears open one end of the protein bar, then brings it down to his crotch, holding it there as though it were his cock.

Oh no, I think, my heart sinking with a sensation of misery that can somehow just as easily be mistaken for pleasure. This is so humiliating. *Please don't tell me ...*

"Go on," he says, giving it a wiggle.

With all abandon thrown behind me like a shirt off my horny back, I get to my knees. Looking up at him one last time, perhaps to ensure that he's not just fucking with me, I then submit to the painfully humiliating (and yet equally erotic and heart-throbbing) process of bowing my head between his firm, shapely jeaned thighs toward that protein bar cock he grips. When my lips meet it, it feels unnatural to bite; my first instinct is to suck it off.

"Don't just *kiss* your dinner." He's toying with me, staring down dominantly as my lips are pressed to his ... bar. "Go on," he encourages me, like I'm some puppy. "Eat."

I bite. The protein bar is stale and gritty. I chew and chew. The hunger in me is so feral, I am far more thankful than I am disgusted with the quality of this cheap—likely 99 cent—bar he got me. All the thousands of dollars they spent today on themselves, and the one and only thing they bought me is this gas-station-variety cheap excuse for a meal replacement.

I am so hungry for Evan.

"Take another bite," he says, licking his lips and watching my every humiliating move. When he speaks, I feel his breath waft over my head. His hot boy breath. His dominance.

His power.

I go for another bite. I'm *so* close to his crotch, to his *real* cock, that I feel blinded with horniness and dizziness—unable to tell those sensations apart anymore. While my head spins, I fight several hundred urges a second to reach up and grab his thighs, to stroke his abs, to cup his firm pecs with my quivering hands; I somehow understand that those impulses are not allowed.

The new houseboy rules, I remind myself.

He makes no effort to help me by tearing the wrapper down further. When I go for the next bite, I have to press with my face to get to the rest of the bar ... which basically means I'm shoving my face deeper and deeper into his crotch, my chin and lips grazing his unhelpful hand. There is something so innately erotic about being lazily fed like a dog by some tough, cute, muscular eighteen-year-old in power. Just the presence of his hand sends shivers of yearning down my body. The hornier I get, the less I seem to notice my other appetite.

He's feeding both my appetites, I realize. *When Evan's here, I'll never hunger, and always hunger.*

When I'm down to the last bite or so, he tosses the wrapper onto the table and keeps in his palm my last remaining bite. When I go to eat it, his hand snaps shut, then begins to knead that final bite in his strong, squeezing fingers while I watch. His fingers open up finally, and all the crumbs and broken bits of that bite lay spread across his palm, mutilated.

"Finish up," he mutters from above.

My insides quiver with excitement as I bring my face to his hand, then slowly begin to lick at every crumb like a dog. I kiss his palm, bringing morsels of protein bar into my mouth. I lick up his finger, licking the chocolate that's smeared there. Feeling braver, I let his whole middle finger into my mouth, sucking grain and chocolate and whatever else is there. I taste the gourmet meal on his fingertips—the one I was *not* allowed to eat—and something about that reminds me of my position, reminds me of what I've been denied, and something deep within me squirms with satisfaction.

I needed this so bad.

Suddenly, he lifts his hand up, pressing it to my face. "Keep going, bitch," I hear him say. My tongue bathes every inch of his hand that I can reach, what with it pressed over my face like a mask. I tongue between his fingers. I slurp and kiss and get all I can from his strong, unrelenting hand.

When he lets go, I'm left suddenly with my face hovering in his crotch, staring down at that perfect alignment of jeans where they fold between his muscular thighs and cup his young, stallion cock. I'm likely lingering here too long, so I pull away and, still on my knees, look up to Evan's eyes expectantly, waiting.

"You have a table to clean up," he tells me. "Then I want you to meet me upstairs in my room. Don't keep me waiting, houseboy."

When he gets up, the side of his ass knocks me in the face unexpectedly, then he saunters out of the dining room heading for the stairs.

I can't get to my feet fast enough. With a speed I didn't know existed in me, I grab all of the dishes and race them to the kitchen. I don't know how Stefan or Jason do it, but I throw them one by one into the dishwasher. I sweep the table of its tablecloth, caring for the crumbs with a haphazard energy that threatens to make a worse mess on the floor than there already is. The tablecloth gets thrown into the washer— no, I don't give a fuck, nor care, nor know what the hell is usually done with table linens—and I turn a blind eye to the rest of the crumbs and mess on the dining room floor. My one and only priority is getting up to Evan's room as fast as humanly possible. *What does he have planned for me next?* I'm shaking all over again, just as I did when I was basically dying from hunger, except this time I'm quavering with the *other* hunger.

I trip three times going up the stairs.

When I reach Evan's door, it's ajar and he's sitting on the bed, poking through one of the bags I'd brought upstairs. He looks up gently, lifting his black eyebrows. "That was quick," he remarks.

"Didn't want to keep you waiting."

"Hope you did a good job, houseboy. Don't want to have to make you clean the whole kitchen and dining room, floor to ceiling."

I want to do that for him. I want him to put me to work and have me suffer sweetly every day. "Did it perfectly," I insist, lying through my teeth and caring not. "You wanted me?"

Evan nods. "I did. See, I've come to another realization." He rises to his feet. The suitcase I'd so delicately packed of all his things rests on the bed. "This room just isn't cutting it."

I frown, genuinely taken aback. "What do you mean? This room's no different than any of the other—"

"Yeah it is." His muscular form draws close to me, so close that I instinctively take a step back. "Get my things, houseboy. We're going to have a ... room reassignment."

With that, he brushes past me, leaving the room. Not wanting to fall behind, I rush to the bed, grab his suitcase and two bags by the foot of the bed, then hurry out of the room to follow him. The bags and suitcase are *not* light. My arms, already sore from the previous lugging of boy-crap from the limo and up the stairs, are pulled mercilessly by their weight. I follow Evan down the hall and around the corner.

He pushes through a door and, to my gut-dropping comprehension, I watch as his eyes drink in the breadth and enormity of my own master bedroom. He strolls in a circle, running his hand along my various cabinets, desks, shoe racks, picture frames, then finally arrives at the door to my attached master bath. "Wow," he remarks, staring inside. "This is considerably bigger than mine ... bigger than any of the boys', really." He peers back at me, his cute, flushed face turning self-satisfied. "I think I'll take this room instead."

"But all my things—" I start to complain.

"Put my stuff on the bed," he orders me, somehow sounding *sweet* in doing so. My heart jumps, drawn to the silkiness of his boyish, sweetly-commanding voice. I *want* to obey his orders, touched and emotional as his words make me. His voice is hypnotic, psychosexual, subliminal, empowering, persuasive.

Despite my aching arms, I lift up and set his heavy suitcase on the bed with due respect. With the two heavy bags, I do the same.

He grins. That grin has fast become the most dangerous thing in the world. "Go back to your room," he says. "I'll get settled in here. I recommend getting plenty of rest, because tomorrow's going to be a long day for you."

It takes me a moment to swallow that sentence because I realize that my room is no longer mine. With a start, I leave him and move down the hall to his old room. My head spins with a million thoughts both logical and chaotically horny as I enter and drop onto the bed. I can't possibly sort these feelings. I think about what he might find in my room. I think about what he might do with my things.

Is this doing him or the boys any good? Or is he taking it too far? Somewhere deep, deep inside of me, I know that I could probably tell him so. I could tell him he's taking it too far, that this is too much, that I wasn't expecting this level of commitment he's taken to teaching me a lesson. He would stop if I asked him to.

That's the real crux of it. I think ... I think I don't *want* him to stop.

I lie on the bed and, in this instant, realize I can still smell him. I close my eyes and inhale deeply, Evan's scent entangling itself in my nostrils and stirring up something from within. A fantasy I haven't yet realized. A dream I never knew. A hole within me I didn't know I had. I just can't get enough of him.

"Enjoying my bed?"

I turn my face, startled to find Evan at the door wearing nothing but jeans. They hang loose on his hips, showcasing those V-shaped muscles that cut down his hips, and the top button is undone, a dusting of his dark pubes peeking out. His chest is cut and chiseled so finely, I literally consider whether this is happening at all or if it's just a dream and some fantasy version of Evan is standing before me. His pink nipples sit on two perfect, perky smooth pecs and his slim eight-pack abs roll like tight little hills, hugging a bellybutton that seems to wink at me from across the room.

"You're fucking gorgeous," I whisper, the only words I can manage to utter.

"I'll let you have my bed," he decides, as though it were a decision he'd made. "But first, I'd like to fuck you on it."

I'm still processing the words he just dared say when suddenly he's climbing up onto the bed and straddling my chest. Instinctively, my hands move away, as though it were illegal to touch his perfect body.

Suddenly, he takes one of my wrists and brings it to the headboard. I stare, confused.

"Where'd you get rope from?" I ask dumbly, watching as he fastens one of my wrists to the bedpost. He doesn't answer and I don't repeat my question. Then he moves to the other wrist and I, a very willing participant in this game of power reversal, let him bind it too.

He moves down to my pants and, with a quick and forceful tug, manages to slip them off my legs as though they were slicked with butter. I even gasp, startled by his strength.

Not to mention that my cock—bone hard and throbbing—points straight up, announcing to the world how very much I'm enjoying this.

He gives my cock a look, then wrinkles his brow. "Wow. For a guy with so much money, you sure have a little dick."

I feel my face start to burn. "It's not *that* small."

"What a little dick for a man." Evan laughs, his voice youthful and light and ringing. With his every laugh, I blush a more furious shade of red. "Little swollen dick. Is that as hard as it gets? That little dick you got?"

"Shut up."

"Shut up?" Evan pulls the zipper of his jeans slowly ... ever slowly. "Shut up?" The zipper drops, drops, drops ... his finger leading it as the jeans separate, split open to reveal more and more of his pubic mound, more and more until the flesh of his buried cock is slowly unveiled as if by the drawing of denim curtains. "Shut up, you said?" The zipper keeps going.

"Sorry," I blurt, staring unblinkingly at his opening crotch.

Then his cock comes out. The size of it puts me to instant shame. I *am* small compared to this powerful, wrestling, dictatorial, keen-as-a-bullet eighteen-year-old who's straddling me like a horse. His cock, easily eight or nine inches, bobs and swells as he holds it in his hand. I've never been more drawn to a cock than I am now. I feel my own throb furiously, pointing and desperate to be touched as I stare at his masterful member.

"I know," he says, his voice almost a moan. "It's amazing. I get it."

"Please," I beg him. "Please, please, please. Evan. I've never wanted anything more. Please. I want it. Please, please, please."

"Yes," he agrees. "And you're paying me to give you what you want, aren't you?"

I swallow hard.

From his back pocket that seems to store everything one might ever conveniently need, he withdraws a grey tube and condom. Rolling on the rubber and squirting the tube's contents on his meat like mustard on a hotdog, he tosses the tube aside and starts jerking off. Then, quite surprisingly, he runs his hand along my crack.

I gasp loudly, attacked by the cold touch of his lubed hand. He says nothing as he works my hole with his wily, merciless fingers. It's only now that I turn my head, noticing that the door's wide-the-fuck-open. Anyone can pass by and see this. Any of the boys could just walk down the hall and pay witness to Evan having his way with me. *This fact would've never mattered to you before,* I tell myself. *Why does it so scare you now?*

When his fingers pull away and the tip of his dick touches me, I gasp, bring my eyes back to meet Evan's, and my whole body tightens. Evan shakes his head. "Nope. Tightening up isn't going to make this pleasant for you."

"I'm not usually—" I swallow again, drunk with my warring desires and fears. "I'm—"

"You're usually the top?" he finishes for me, flippant. "You're paying me a great deal to work for you. Part of that, I imagine, includes putting you sexually beneath me. Doesn't it?" I don't answer. He takes my non-answer for a yes. "I think that means my cock is going inside of you tonight. You're going to feel my cock inside you, pushing you apart, splitting you in half. I'm going to fuck you until you're screaming my name, houseboy."

I've never felt this mixture of equal parts horniness and fear. Can I even *take* him inside me? Is this even physically possible? Is it going to hurt? Is it going to be fucking amazing?

"Don't you want to get your money's worth?" he asks, and then a wicked grin pushes his rosy cheeks into those burning blue eyes that I've worshipped since the day I discovered his application on the kitchen counter.

He thrusts his cock. I resist my urge to fight him and, despite the muscles in my body flexing, I feel him slip in. I breathe deep, my hands pulling the rope he's bound them with taut. My mouth hanging open, I stare at him in disbelief. I can't believe he's inside me.

"That's just the tip," Evan whispers, as if reading my thoughts.

Then he begins to hump my ass, slowly thrusting his tip in and out of me, massaging my hole with his thick, swollen manhood. I am about to move my legs when suddenly he grips either one with his powerful hands, lifting the entirety of my ass and hips off the bed. I've literally handed him my ass, helpless to resist. Holding me up, his beautiful arms and pecs flex ferociously, gleaming in the soft light pouring off the sconces on the wall. *It's illegal for a boy so beautiful to exist. It's simply fucking illegal.* He carries my lower half and gently pushes and pushes and pushes that cock, massaging my ass into a state of helpless invitation.

My body begins to relax. I feel my muscles working down there, stretching, releasing, and his cock slips further in with each thrust. It is so erotic, so sensual, so ... sensitive ... that I might almost trick myself into believing that Evan cares for me. I stare into his blue eyes, searching for a sign. *He's being so tender with you,* I realize. *He doesn't want to hurt you.*

"That's still just the tip," he has to tell me, playing with my psyche, toying with me, fucking my mind as innocently as he's fucking my body. "You'll scream my name, houseboy."

He pushes in further. I gasp, overcome.

I thought he'd entered me before; I was dead wrong. Naked only from the waist down, my shirt bunched up around my chest and armpits, I pull against the ropes as he thrusts deeper and deeper into me, his firm grip on my legs threatening to put them to sleep. I'm defenseless in his powerful grapple, trapped in a high school wrestler's submission hold without a hope—or desire—of twisting free. *Oh, to be trapped in those thighs of yours, Evan.* My best and worst wrestling fantasies swim to the surface as his cock pushes further and further into me. *Keep going, Evan. Fuck the money out of me. Fuck the monster out of me. Fuck the selfishness and the greed and the solitude out of me.*

Then, unexpectedly, he lurches forward and this whole experience becomes quite sobering and real. He lets go, presses his hands into the bed as he's leaned forward, my legs propped up at his shoulders. Boy-in-charge Evan fucks me hard. The bed protesting against each and every thrust, I find myself moaning and rasping with his firm, muscular movements. The ropes burn into my wrists and my legs dangle helplessly.

"You're my houseboy," he whispers, his eyes burning and his words made jagged by the ferocious fucking. "You're just my houseboy. You're my toy, Liam ... You're my *toy*."

"Yes, boss!" I breathe back, hardly able to find breath with which to utter said words.

When he cums, I feel everything.

He exhales over my face, his hot breath pouring with his sexual relief. The thrusts stop as the cum rockets out of his pulsing cock. My vision watery and blurred, my lips dry from all the heavy breathing, I can't see anything for a long while but the swirling semidarkness of sex and stars.

Then his face comes into view: pretty and blue-eyed, a spiky mess of sopping-wet black hair on his forehead. His lazy smile tells the tale of his satisfaction without uttering a word.

"That was so hot," I breathe.

His eyes come to focus, pulled from the trance his orgasm drew him into. "I suspect you'd like to cum, too."

"Please," I beg him. "I'm so horny."

"Yeah," he agrees, his cock slipping out of me. "So horny." He steps off the bed, yanks the condom off and flings it at my trash. I don't even know if it made it. "So very horny." Over his cum-dripping, still-hard cock, he pulls up his opened jeans.

"Evan ..."

"And we should always get what we want," he says, his blue eyes turning dark.

I realize he's about to leave me. "Evan!"

His reddened face glows with that all-familiar post-orgasm heaven. "Sweet dreams, houseboy," he sings, then saunters out the door.

"Evan!" I cry, screaming out his name just as promised, but not as expected. My stiffy points to the ceiling and throbs with each futile thrust of my hips. My hands bound, I can't reach it at all. Evan's gone, left me wrestling with my worst opponent yet: a pent-up cock, untouched, with no means whatsoever of relief.

[10]

I wake to a tickling sensation at my right hand. When I open an eye, I find Zac's stoic form by the bed, gently undoing my binds.

"Zac," I manage to say.

He doesn't respond, releasing my wrists one at a time from the bed. When the first is free, I draw my hand to my chest protectively. He comes around the bed to undo the other. When it too falls, I massage my wrists and sit up, wary. I must've fallen right asleep after Evan left even despite being hard as a rock, so ridiculously exhausted as I was.

Zac says nothing after his duty's finished.

He just passes like a ghost out of the wide-open door. Was it left open all night? Did any of the boys, even out of mere curiosity, pass by my room and stare at their half-naked boss on the bed bound by his wrists?

First thing I do is push into my bathroom—Evan's old bathroom—and pee forever. Forever and ever and ever and ever. The world spins and, quite suddenly, the fantasy of it all passes and all I'm left with is a ringing in my left ear, sore wrists, a crick in my neck, and a growling tummy.

Donning the pair of pants off the floor that were so aggressively thrust off by Evan last night, I step out of my room and, feeling dirty, slowly come down the stairs. When I pass by the living room, I find many of the boys in front of the TV playing the PS4. Everything seems so like usual that I wonder if it's all over. One night of horniness. One night of madness. One night of a sexual fantasy gone wrong.

Is that the end of it? Is Evan finished and we're all returned to our posts?

I stalk to the kitchen, tired, sore, and still massaging my wrists. Opening the fridge, I help myself to anything I can find. When I push a cube of cheese into my lips, it's gone before I taste it. I pull out one of the dishes from last night onto the counter, then drop into a stool and help myself to leftovers. The more I eat, the hungrier I realize I am.

And when my stomach's fed, the logic and the reality of things seem to reoccur to me, much like waking from a dream. Evan's had his fun with me. I've pulled the beast out of him somehow and he spent a good day unleashing it on me. He had his fun, but so did I. Even now the morning after, the sensations of excitement and thrill swim in my belly. Part of me even wants more, somehow. Is this even within his character, to do such cruel things to a person? He was so nice when I first let him into my limo that day ...

"Hungry boy."

I look up. Evan's leaning against the wall, arms crossed, and he's smiling at me. That smile no longer means what it used to. I can't see through the mask of character he's put on anymore. Who is Evan? Is he a cruel boy playing a role, or is he the sweet kid I've invited onto my staff?

"You wanna keep going?" he asks.

I lift a brow. "What do you mean? With the cruelty and the ... treating me like I'm the scum of your shoe?"

He laughs lightly, gives a shrug. "Come on. I wasn't *that* bad to you, was I?"

My eyes draw down his body, studying his shape through the loose t-shirt he's got on. The sound of his soft breathing as he awaits my answer brings my mind back to last night when he had me in the palm of his hand. Literally, licking out of it. I wonder if I'll ever see a boy past his clothes and his body, into the parts that matter ... the parts that people come to relate to and love and write songs about.

"Truth is," I say, meeting his eyes finally, "I'm not sure any amount of cruelty's going to teach me the lesson I deserve."

Evan's eyes soften instantly. He comes to the counter, leaning across it the way Preston always does, and the evilness of his smirk is gone. "You think I overdid it?"

"No."

"What's wrong, then?"

"I'm afraid I enjoyed it too much."

He lifts his eyebrows, surprised by my statement. I find myself looking down quite suddenly, like I'm as surprised by my words as he. Unexpectedly, he reaches to my cheek and gives it a little pop with his hand. "Chin up, Liam. You're still my boss. I'm still your boy. What we did yesterday, that was just us all having fun. The money's just a drop in the bucket to you, isn't it? Besides, I can return it all. Except for the protein bar, since you kinda ate it." I crack a smile and try quite badly to hide it. "We were playing yesterday."

"Felt a bit more than playing," I reason, picking at my nails. "Felt like my life had just somehow ... changed. In one instant. In one night. I was a completely different person. I was at your feet. I was eating out of your lap. I was fucked like some kind of ... sex toy."

"Isn't that what you want?" Evan comes around the counter, unsettling me for a second until he's come to rest in the seat to my side. I look up, wondering if the stirring in my heart at his closer presence is from desire or fear. "I didn't turn all hardcore on you to hurt you, Liam. I did it because you—"

"Because I treat the boys like meat," I say to spare him answering. "Because I—what did you say?—I surround myself with beautiful boys who I can ogle at all the time. I'm like the old man whose lawn you used to mow except I don't offer lemonade. I provide something far less sweet, but perhaps as tart."

"What's that?"

I look deep into the recesses of my soul, and no matter how hard I strain, I can't see my dad on the beach, or around a firepit, or resting in a big cushy bed in Heaven. He's nowhere to be found. He's gone.

"Money," I answer.

Evan smirks. "I think the sweetness of that is fairly debatable."

"I'm confused, Evan. I don't know what it is I need. I don't know if this arrangement is ... is going to work."

I sigh. I strain again to search through the darkness inside me. Why can't I see my dad? Why isn't he smirking at me with that told-you-so look I always imagine him having?

"You like me," Evan says. "Right?"

I can't even bring myself to look at him again, staring at and fidgeting with my hands. I can't look at his thick thighs, hugged by a pair of sexy new jeans he obviously got yesterday. I can't look at his pecs, gracefully caressed by that loose shirt he's got on. I can't even allow myself the pleasure of a racing heart by looking upon his sculpted arms, thick shoulders, or sexy hands that have, alone, granted me so much pleasure. I feel like some assumed permission to enjoy these things has been revoked somehow.

"And I mean more than cupcakes," he goes on, leaning in as if to get in my face. "You like me a lot. The boys told me as much. Even Zac told me how insistent you were on bringing me into the house. I know you're into me."

"What's your point, Evan?" I say this to my hands, patiently forcing myself to hear him out, to give him at least that.

"You like Preston, right? You like Jason and Madison and the others? You like Kyle?"

"Of course I like my boys."

"Then you ought to trust them, too." Evan puts a hand on my shoulder. He starts to rub slowly, gently, massaging my shoulder. A shiver of pleasure runs through my body, and it follows in waves with every push and pull and squeeze of his skilled hand. "They've all known you long enough. Some more than others. They know what you like. Trust them. Maybe you shouldn't always be the one in control, Liam."

"I don't know. I'm not sure I can handle what you and the others did to me yesterday, every day. Sometimes I need kindness. There are days when I just need ..." A buddy? Cuddles? Love? *What is it you want, Liam? Do you even know* how *to love, you miserable, depraved fool?*

"Every relationship's different," Evan says, juggling with my logic. "Don't judge what we have, or what it is you like. Sometimes a relationship goes wrong and has to end. Other times, the strangest relationship can work. Even a very ... unconventional one. What's the harm if everyone's happy? Sometimes you like it mean. Sometimes you like it sweet. You take care of us, Liam. You give us a home. This is the best fucking summer I've ever had. Now let *us* take care of *you.*"

Those words send another chill down my body that's nothing to do with his hand, which still works my shoulder over with ease. *Now let us take care of you.* Oh, the countless dark, naughty, torturous, exciting and *horrible* things he can be implying with those innocent words. Does a person like me even deserve such care?

"Take care of me," I repeat back to him, tasting the words. "How, exactly, are you and the boys going to accomplish that?"

Still rubbing my shoulder, his thumb digging into it with such strength that I resist moaning, he brings his other hand to my face, turning it toward his. I'm inches from his deep, beautiful blue eyes. His black hair jabs across his forehead in messy, unorganized tufts. His cheeks are flushed adorably, and the teeth that show in his cocky smile are bright.

To my eyes, he says, "Some days we play nice. Some days we don't."

Unexpectedly, his lips draw forth and connect with mine. I shut my eyes and inhale deeply—a gasp, almost. His lips are incredibly soft and feverish. His hand still gripping my shoulder, I feel his energy so easily in just this light, nothing kiss. I feel it like a gut feeling. I'm stirred within, a tangle of excited, confused emotions using my body like a bouncy castle.

He pulls away. "There's no guarantee this will work," he tells me with a little shrug, "but I'm willing to give it a try."

Maybe I don't need my dad watching from the darkness within. Maybe he's let me go.

"With nice days and not-so-nice days," I say back. He gives one slow nod. I squint into those eyes of his. "And what kind of day is today, if I may ask?"

Letting go of my face, his free hand dives downward, grabbing a surprisingly firm and well-aimed grip of my crotch. I gasp, drop my jaw, and watch his face turn devilish.

With a rush of desire and staring into those baby blues, I find the answer I was hoping for.

[11]

The morning Evan leaves for his first day of college, it's a "nice" day. Some of the boys are doing their usual thing playing video games in the living room while Zac helps carry Evan's backpack down the stairs. When Zac pushes out the door to take his backpack to the limo, Evan finds me leaning patiently against the archway by the grand stairs.

He's wearing an outfit I bought him: a handsomely-fitted maroon shirt with distressed grey jeans, crinkled at the ankles by solid white athletic shoes. He looks smart and fresh and ready as hell to hit his first day of classes.

"I hate doctors," I tell him.

Evan grins. "Even young, sexy ones? Don't tell me if I was the one in the white coat who came into the room that you wouldn't quite suddenly change your opinion on that."

"You worked a certain kind of surgery on my life, I suppose." I give him a onceover, my eyes drawing a line down his young body. I wonder if he'll meet anyone on campus. He will be around so many like-minded, driven guys. This is such an important time in his life and I want him to succeed. "Jury's still out on whether or not this patient is fixed."

"Some things are meant to stay broken," he says, giving my nipple a playful pinch through my shirt. I pull away with a chuckle, rubbing it. "They're more beautiful that way."

"Aww, Evan. You calling me beautiful?"

"You always were ... for an old man."

Evan laughs, and I scowl playfully at him. Why do I feel like I'm saying goodbye? He'll be back tonight after classes. The campus is just half an hour away. He's commuting.

"Make smart choices," I tell him, giving Evan a pat on his shoulder.

He comes in for a hug instead. I feel his body as he grips me tight, caressing me. Too reluctant to return the hug at first, I just stand there for a moment, my arms out, unsure where to put them. I wonder if I'll ever work out the puzzle of lust and love, of what lives between them, if anything. Can anything touch me within but the sight of muscles and beautiful blue eyes? What is the broken thing inside of me that never seems able to be fixed?

I return the hug tightly, all my unanswered questions squished between us and his pair of muscled pecs and his firm abs against mine. The hug is so tight, even our hips connect.

When he pulls away, he gives me a kiss on the cheek, then says, "I'll be back for dinner. Have it ready and hot for me, houseboy." And then, with a final wink, he heads out the door to catch up to Zac.

I watch through the window, observing the sight of the young, musclebound boy I dared to bring into my house. His meaty butt wags left and right delectably as he strolls down the curved walkway to the waiting limo. Mixed with a dark hunger and a sick yearning and an excitement I can't in any way name, I watch through the glass until his beautiful shape disappears into the limo, until it growls to life, then rides down the driveway and out of sight.

The sound of futuristic gunfire, explosions, and aliens screaming in discord draws me to the living room where the backs of Preston's and Madison's heads poke up from the couch. As if by some psychic connection—or perhaps by the sound of my bare feet padding across the foyer—Preston's tousled head of bleach blonde hair whips around, and those rich green eyes find mine.

For a moment, I'm frozen in place by the intensity of his stare. With the wicked playing of minds and sex and cocks and power that has so driven me wild over the last month since Evan began his routine on-and-off torment of me, I never know what state I'll find my boys in. Some days it's nice, some days it's cruel. One day, the boys surprised me by serving dinner on Preston's smooth, naked body. Of course, when I finished, I gave him a kiss on the lips, finding them to be the tastiest of all. We all laughed when he got an erection halfway through dinner, and Madison gave it a playful jerking, causing Preston to squirm. Another day was cruel, with the boys making me rub their feet during the entire course of a movie they all kicked back to watch, Kyle included. I was quite excited when I reached his feet, strong and warm. He huffed, looking down the length of his ripped body to watch me as I worked his toes. Near the end of the movie, he turned me into a footrest. The next week, we staged a tournament of naked oil wrestling in the backyard. I insisted that I only judge and not participate, but Evan pulled off my clothes and pitted me against Preston, and the two of us slipped and slid all over the place. Everyone burst into laughter when I tumbled to my face. Preston caught me in a submission hold despite our slippery bodies. He demanded I give and accept defeat, and I defied him, hungrily, suffering under his powerful pin. When my boner was acknowledged, the tournament turned into something else entirely and the oil was, to say the least, *helpful*.

I watch Preston's piercing gaze as he stares at me from the couch. The smartness in his sharp green eyes either means he's ready to pounce, or curious about what I'd like for lunch today. It's hard to tell which days are nice ones and which days are not.

But, to be really honest, I just want to be welcomed without a fee. I want to be a part of someone's atmosphere. No, even more than that. I want to *be* someone's atmosphere. I want to be on their mind. I want to be wanted ... without having to beg for it. Or pay.

Preston lifts a brow, and almost impatiently he says, "Saved a spot for you!" He pats the cushion of couch between him and Madison. "Get your butt over here!"

"I ... don't wanna disturb your game."

"You kidding? You're playing in our next match." Preston gives his buddy a shove, which is returned with a deep grunt and a mumbled expletive. "Madison needs to have his ass handed to him. C'mon, Liam. You and I are gonna be on a team."

A warm sensation floods my insides. It's something like the first hot breath of spring after a winter that's frozen the world solid.

"I've never played," I confess, drawing up to the couch. When I'm about to sit, Preston yanks suddenly on my waistband, pulling me into my place on the couch with such force that I have to laugh.

"No better time to learn than the present!" he exclaims, grinning into my face. I return his grin with a hesitant one of my own, and then a third game controller is slapped into my unready hands. "Prepare yourself, teammate."

Preston shows me the controls, taking his time. Wow, Preston smells very nice today. He makes sure to laugh and make fun of me each time I press the wrong button and blow my character up or send a missile into the sky. He was always the sweetest of them all, Preston.

"Ready?" he asks before our match begins.

"No," I answer, but it starts anyway, and before long, I'm thrust headlong into a whole new game, and it's full of fun and danger. I'll make mistakes. I'll fuck things up. I'll guffaw at the dumbest little things. I'll spit out the drink I'm sipping on and slap Madison on the back, forgetting who's on whose team. I'll shove my shoulder into Preston's, giggling, giving him sidelong glances and sharing joys and worries and laughter as we play some game that I might never succeed at ... some game that might always feel new and unfamiliar ... some game where I'll always have someone at my side.

And really, isn't that how the fuck it should always be?

The end.

Printed in Great Britain
by Amazon